SHE WRITES ENTERTAINMENT PRESENTS

A NOVEL BY

SHEENA HEROD

SHEwrites
ENTERTAINMENT

ISBN: 978-1-64854-999-1 (Paperback)
ISBN: 978-1-64854-998-4 (eBook)

Front cover image by Marion Designs www.mariondesigns.com

SYNOPSIS

The saying goes, "you have to pay the cost to be a boss"

At eighteen, Destiny seemed to have her entire life together, thriving in her first semester at UOM on scholarship, with hopes of making it to the WNBA. However, like everybody who's out to make money in Memphis, Destiny lands in trouble with a professional NBA player by the name of D. Wallace. He gives her a shot at the good life but being the woman of a ball player comes with rules.

When the relationship goes from good to nothing, Destiny must learn how to make it in the world alone by playing life by her rules. However, Destiny soon realizes that she must make bigger moves and sort out major plans to make more money. Then she lands in the presence of Jackson, a man who is a friend of the rich and fortunate.

Jackson makes big promises and finds a doorway into Destiny's heart. After being hurt once, Destiny isn't too thrilled with the way she falls head over heels for Jackson.

But to her, money always had the privilege of talking, and that's what she was after.

Follow Destiny as she learns the value of family, the evil that comes with money, and what is required to keep her status.

Four Years Ago

CHAPTER *One*

The view of the Mississippi River was poetry in landscape form. The sun shined through the thin layer of clouds and caused the sky to appear golden orange in color. Not many were able to bask in the beauty of Memphis during those hours because they were either rushing to clock in at their jobs or arriving home from being in the streets heavy. The only aspect locals could see was the violence and pain the city brought. They witnessed innocents being locked away or the bums on the street corners standing wide-eyed as they waited for their next hit of a crack pipe, along with the drug dealers shooting down another one of the hood's own.

Unlike most people who lived in the city, Destiny tried to rise above the environment by working her way up to the WNBA league. Although sometimes it seemed like a dream, she had already received a full-ride scholarship from the University of Memphis to play college basketball.

She was one step closer to living the dream, however, money still was an issue, and as the saying goes, *it made the world go around.* Where Destiny grew up, money made people or broke them down to their knees, there was never a line between.

Destiny rose with something heavy on her spirit. All she knew was that things had to change. She grew tired of rubbing pennies together to afford her next meal. She could never have a good day at school and then come home to a hot cooked meal because her mother was one hit of a crack rock from the grave. No matter how many times Destiny begged her mother, Tammy, to stop, and go to rehab, it didn't work. Her begging normally resulted in Tammy spiraling, so now all Destiny did was try her best to stay out of the way.

"Bitchhh!" Destiny heard her best friend, Dominique, enter the house.

Usually, Dominique paid a visit when she knew Destiny had settled in at home after a long day of classes and basketball practice. Back in high school, which was only a summer ago, they used to meet up every evening. But those evenings eventually fell through the cracks when Destiny enrolled in a better school. Which was the result of her varsity coach Mrs. Miller who saw the potential in Destiny and knew that she would only thrive if she was given the opportunity to get away from her previous school.

"What?" Destiny raised from the bed with a confused expression.

She figured it had to be serious business if Dominique was there early in the morning. She hadn't brushed her teeth or taken care of hygiene, and Dominique was there all amped as if she'd won the lottery.

"Damn! Bitch you need to buy some air freshener in this house. Your momma smell like she walked out of the graveyard." Dominque threw her hands in the air and focused on Destiny.

"That's not why I'm here though."

"Then why are you here?"

Destiny viewed Dominque from the bit of distance that lay between them. Dominque gave a devilish grin then placed both of her hands on her hips as Destiny stood in anticipation.

"Some of the players from the Miami Heats are supposed to be at the spot tonight after the game with the Grizzlies." Dominque laid the information on Destiny like she had told her she got a one-way ticket to Heaven and God himself would greet her at the pearly gates.

Destiny dropped her head in disappointment, there was always something up with Dominque. She never tried to earn a living the right way. And at only eighteen, she had it already mapped out how she was going to get out of the hood. It had nothing to do with hard work either, it was set in stone within her being that she would get wifed up by a baller or be a side woman to one. Either way, she wouldn't have to struggle the way she saw her momma and aunts do over the years.

"Ughhh!" Destiny let out a loud sigh.

She walked around the room a bit, she pulled clothes from every direction, trying to piece together something to wear to school.

"I'm so tired of going to these damn games and clubs trying to get these niggas' attention when every groupie in Memphis is there trying to do the same damn thing—trying to grab a fuckin' bag."

"Nahhh, bitch! We in there this time. My brother-in-law's cousin, Tracey's boyfriend, is the promoter. So, we for sure will get next to the ballers. VIP access," Dominique said with confidence.

Destiny stopped the task at hand. "You sure we gettin' in?"

"Yesss, bitch! We are in there don't even sweat it. Besides, I need a real come-up. I'm so tired of these fake balling as Memphis niggas. Out of town niggas is where the money at, and that's what we're gon' get." Dominque flopped on the bed and laid out flat as she viewed the ceiling.

"I can't believe you got us a spot in VIP. Like you really came through this fuckin' time like you said you would," Destiny said.

"Girl, yes, we about to be around a different breed of niggas from the ones around here. All these niggas do is steal and kill. I met one nigga who claimed he fix credit on the side. Then he had the nerve to ask for my social—

claiming he could get me loans. I'm like nigga, for real, you think I'm going to give you my info?" Dominque raised from the bed after being down one minute too long.

"Yeap, that's them. Always up to some bullshit. But at least you got a nice ass

car from one of them niggas. I'm still riding around in a car that has the engine light on," Destiny said.

Before that encounter with Dominique, Destiny bumped the thought of being with an NBA player, because she had it instilled in her mind that she was going to get drafted in the WNBA and have a nice living herself if she received the opportunity to play ball overseas.

"Shit, that's all I got. I'm ready for a real change. You will have a nice car too when we grab a ballplayer tonight."

Dominique sat upright on the bed; she took a good view of Destiny's room. Not much had changed over the years, except Destiny now had one too many trophies lined up on her wall along with metals. Dominique never could understand why Destiny took basketball seriously. She saw it easier getting bread from somebody who was already up rather than working too damn hard with no surety that a reward was behind the hard work.

"You and this damn basketball thing is killing me. Like, let that shit go already. You good and shit sure enough, but you working too fucking hard when all you have to do is find the right nigga." Dominique stood from the bed. She strolled over to the door and leaned against the feeble frame.

"What basketball thing?" Destiny's blood boiled.

Dominique, of all people, knew that basketball was life to Destiny. It kept Destiny out of trouble and saved her from all the mess Tammy got in over the years. She was sure that if she kept at it, it would change her life forever. She was already all in the papers around Memphis. People knew her and not because she was some man's girl. She was getting praise due to the simple fact of her loving the sport.

"Because I love it. You should know that. Besides, this is my sure meal ticket out of this city."

Destiny placed a pink t-shirt, and a pair of storm-washed jeans on the bed, along with a pink Nike head-band. It wasn't any expensive outfit, however, it at least looked decent enough to wear out in public.

"Nah, gettin' a rich nigga is the answer. And how do you think you gon' catch a baller playing ball and always at the gym? Guys don't want no sweaty pussy." Dominique smacked her lips and made a sound that caused Destiny to repel her.

"I got to get dressed for school. I'll holla at you later." Destiny kindly showed Dominque the way out as if she hadn't been there more than anyone could count.

"Damn, okay. Kick a bitch out like that, huh?" Dominique turned from the doorframe and followed behind Destiny with her lips puckered.

She came off too demanding sometimes, it caused Destiny to get in her feelings. She figured what kind of friend she would be if she didn't give her homegirl the uncut truth? That's what good friends did, they made sure they spoke the truth regardless of how it made the next one feel, at least that was her logic of the situation.

Destiny stopped in her tracks and turned to Dominique. If Destiny didn't know how to do anything, she knew how to defend herself whenever someone tried to make her feel small. Basketball taught her how to have tough skin, and allow what others say to roll off like sweat. At the end of the day, the only opinions that mattered were the coaches. She took their word everywhere she went. No one's opinions matter if they weren't trying to get her to the next level.

"And for your information, I can do both." Destiny turned back around and kept in her tracks. She swung the flimsy wooden door open and shooed Dominique out.

"You know I'm on a scholarship for college. If I stop playin' I can't go to school. I'm trying to make a way. If a nigga with money happens to come my way or I fall into his life, that's cool too, but I want my own shit too to fall back on."

Dominique threw her hands in the air, clearly over the conversation of Destiny's hoop dream. She had bigger shit to worry about. Like what she was going to wear to the party and making sure she chose the right time to leave out so they wouldn't be late. She learned firsthand that the worse that could happen was showing up after the ballers were already in the spot. By then one too many bitches had shown their faces.

"Okay, whatever girl. Just don't be late. I'm tryin' to get there at a decent time, so I'm the first sexy face they see walk in." Dominique pressed the button on the remote to unlock the door to her all-white Land Rover.

"So, you can be the first? You must forget I'm walking in too, huh?" Destiny said in a confident tone.

"I haven't forgotten shit. You will be the second sexy face they see," Dominque said as she sucked her teeth.

"Yeah, whatever." Destiny brushed Dominique's words off once more.

Once they reached the edge of the driveway, Destiny stopped in route and allowed Dominique to walk ahead. Dominque strolled past a few cars that were parked on side of the road before she reached hers then she hopped in. She rolled the window down before pulling away from the curve.

"Don't make us late tonight, bitchhh!" Dominique pulled off. Before long, her SUV was out of sight.

Destiny shook her head in deep thought; she knew that Dominique was right in some ways. She needed a Plan B to her plans. Making it to the WNBA and playing overseas wasn't a sure thing. Sure enough, she was putting in hard work. There were many other women out there working their asses off too. Sometimes that very fact didn't give her much hope with the whole pro thing.

Destiny walked into the house and her eyes fell on Tammy on the couch in an old blue, dirty robe surrounded by a cloud of cigarette smoke. Normally she slept in long after Destiny left the house, that day was different.

"Oh, hi momma," Destiny greeted, trying her best to get the hell out of sight.

"You have people over here too damn early. All that loud ass talkin' like nobody isn't in the bed trying to fuckin' sleep. That's what's wrong with ya ass now, you think the world revolves around your black ass." Tammy pulled her robe tighter around the frame that used to be a slight bit heavier and much healthier too.

"First of all, I don't ever have people over here early. And today was an exception. Dominique had something important to tell me. I didn't think you would be able to hear anything since drugs have you fucked up most of the time." Destiny gave Tammy the attitude right back.

During Destiny's earlier years, she tried her best to be respectful to her mother, but then Destiny realized that her mother didn't even have respect for herself, so why should she?

"Sick of your smart-ass mouth. You can get out of my damn house with all that. Ya ass is eighteen anyway. Hell, I don't know why you still here." Tammy took a drag of the stale cigarette; she charged it to her lungs and then released it.

"You can get the fuck out. I won't miss your lil stank, high-yella ass anyway." Tammy grabbed a magazine from the old end table and tossed it at Destiny with force.

"Bitch!"

Destiny moved out of the way and dodged it. She learned at an early age that she had to be quick in order to get out of the way of Tammy's rage. One minute it would be a magazine, the next it would be a pan.

"I wish I had a momma who actually gave fuck about

my life then maybe things would be easier. But no, I'm out there trying to make some out of myself while you in here constantly beating me emotionally to my knees. Then you pull this shit, throwing stuff at me." Destiny punched the wall and regretted it once the pain shot from her knuckles up to her forearm.

"Not scared of you anymore, Tammy. I'm not afraid of the shit you do or say. Maybe if you go get another crack rock, you'll calm the fuck down. That's what you like to do, right, momma? You like to get high off crack and forget the world around you?"

"Don't worry about what I do and what I like to do or how I like to feel." Tammy put out the cigarette in the scummy ashtray.

"You don't pay bills here. All you do is bounce a basketball when you should bounce your stupid ass around the city and get a fuckin' job."

"Whatever, Tammy."

Destiny stormed to the back to get dressed for school. She had a lot on her plate with college, plus she had an upcoming game that WNBA scouts were going to attend. The drama she dealt with at home had to take a back seat for a while.

After classes let out for the day, Destiny made her way to the University gym for practice with Shirell, a friend she made when she first stepped foot at UOM. Shirell and her were basically from the same tracks, but different hoods. Shirell didn't come from much, and although her mother wasn't some crack addict, her father was an alcoholic and was in and out of her life. All she wanted was to make a better living for herself and possibly get her mother out of the hood.

"You got me in here when coach gave us the day off. You going to overwork the both of us." Shirell passed the ball to Destiny, then Destiny passed the ball back to Shirell. They repeated the process until Destiny moved on to floor drills.

"I want to make sure I'm ready for the next game. You know if you want to be the best, you have to work twice as hard."

Destiny dribbled the ball. The way she moved fascinated Shirell. She always got that way whenever Destiny was on the court. She knew deep in her soul that if Destiny really stuck to it, she was going places that no other female player in the city ever went.

"What you got up this weekend?" Destiny made an all-net, three-pointer jump shot.

"Hell, yeah." Destiny basked in her perfect shot as she walked over to the sideline.

"Not shit tonight. I have to study…you know finals and shit is coming up. I'm trying to make sure these grades look good." Shirell took a seat on the bleachers as Destiny followed suit.

"Girl, you are always in the books. You need to loosen up some and have a bit of fun." Destiny tried to stop herself in midsentence, she sounded more like Dominque with each passing day.

"Yeah, because I'm trying to transfer out of here—don't get me wrong, it's a good school. I'm trying to get to someplace better," Shirell replied.

Destiny popped her head to the side; it was her first hearing about Shirell trying to transfer out. They weren't best friends; however, they were close. They talked about a lot in the short amount of time they had been friends.

"Man, I plan on going to Atlanta to play at Georgia State," Shirell said.

Destiny frowned. "Why are you trying to leave? You got it good here."

"How the hell I got it good? Because I'm in college? Nah, if that's the case, you got it good, too." Shirell shook her head. Her dream had always been to get far away from Memphis, go somewhere deep in the south and thrive.

"I'm only here because I know how to ball. My grades alone wouldn't have gotten me here. The teachers really tampered with a lot of tests to see me here. Hell, sometimes I don't even feel like I deserve any of this—Like maybe I don't belong here after all."

Destiny dropped her head; she thought back on the argument she had with Tammy that morning. She figured maybe it was time to let the dream die and get a job to cover some bills and be able to afford nicer things.

Shirell patted Destiny on the back and sighed. "You definitely should be here."

"You really going to leave, huh?"

Destiny didn't get along with most of the players on the team. They felt like they were competing for the leading spot. All Destiny wanted to do was play ball and make better. The players on the team wanted to be seen and have a name amongst Memphis. Unknowingly she was living their dream.

"Yeah, it doesn't matter what side of town you live on in Memphis it's no success here. Too many people hate and try to kill you for being successful. Besides, Atlanta is where young black people can shine. Black money and black power. And that's what I want." Shirell threw her fist in the air to represent black power.

She made it sound like another world, the whole Atlanta thing. Destiny heard of the thriving black community in Atlanta, the way Shirell described it made it sound like black heaven.

"That sounds like the place to be." Destiny raised from the bleacher. She grabbed her gym bag and tossed it over her shoulder. "The only thing I need to be successful is being a baller and pulling a baller that got baller money."

Shirell frowned as the words hit her. Destiny bragged on how she was going to make things happen with her basketball career. Shirell never really heard her talk about some rich man being her meal ticket. She knew with

Destiny having a friend like Dominique, she would soon become like her, if not worse, if she didn't find a way to think for herself.

"You starting to sound like Dominique. That chick needs a serious reality check and get out more if that's all she is thinking about. You're better than some rich man taking care of you and controlling your life." Shirell grabbed her gym bag and followed Destiny. She had to make it home to study and get focused, while Destiny had to make it to the other side of the city to meet Dominique at her house to get dressed.

Destiny continued her path out of the gym. She refused to take any of Shirell's words seriously. She had to make something happen regardless.

"Speaking of gettin' out, why don't you come to the club with me and Dominique tonight? Find you a rich nigga, so you don't have to worry about moving away," Destiny said.

"Nah, you go have fun with your lil homegirl. You already know she's not the type of chick I like to be around." Shirell declined the offer.

"Alright, fine." Destiny said before she and Shirell departed in the parking lot.

It was a little past seven o'clock. Destiny was already behind schedule in Dominque's eyes, it literally took hours for them to get ready on a simple day. An occasion like trying to bag ballers was considered the main event, they had to dress their best which required more effort with picking out attire.

CHAPTER *Two*

Destiny pulled into the driveway next to Dominique's Land Rover. She threw the gear in park and snatched the key out of the switch in one go. She grabbed her bag out of the front seat and darted out of the car as her life depended on it. Dominique had been blowing her phone up since she pulled out of the parking lot at UOM. Destiny told her that it wouldn't take her long to head over there. Traffic was still thick, which made the commute longer.

Destiny hadn't even made it in the house good, Dominique snatched her up and made her shower. When she exited the shower, there was already an outfit picked out for her, not something she would've picked out herself. The entire outfit looked like Dominique. Once she was dressed, Dominque did her makeup, and they were out the door at the speed of light.

They made their way to the front of the club only to spot a line nearly down the street to the next block. The crowd consisted mostly of women. Dominique didn't expect anything less since most of the women in Memphis were trying to get their hands on the rich men that were there visiting.

"Yo what's up with this line? I thought we didn't have to wait?" Destiny viewed the line with wide eyes. She knew that if they had to wait in a line like that, they weren't ever going to get close to any baller.

Dominique grabbed her phone out of her small MK purse and called the promoter. She looked around with an uneasy expression. There was no way she would wait the line out after being promised VIP access to rich men.

"Hold that shit what you talkin' about. I'm trying to get this nigga on the phone right now."

Dominique walked over to the front entrance with Destiny following her closely in the highest heels she ever wore. Anyone who knew Destiny knew she wasn't a fan of high heels, she liked gym shoes and all things tomboys liked. That wasn't an option that night if she wanted to be seen.

"Excuse me handsome, I'm looking for Big L....the promoter." Dominique batted her eyelashes seductively at the bouncer who could pass as Biggie Smalls' twin.

"I don't know where he is lil mama but you got to get to the back of the line. That's the rule," the bouncer said in a deep voice.

"No, you don't understand, I'm a special guest of his.

He personally invited me." Dominique tried her best to set things straight. Big L promised her, and he had always been good on his word.

"Yea and three hundred other chicks. Get in line." the bouncer shooed Dominique away like she was a fly that kept trying to land on him.

"No, I'm not no damn three hundred other chicks. I should be on a damn list or something," Dominique smacked her lips. She had it set in her mind that she was going to land in the arms of a rich man. Some bouncer wasn't going to stand in the way of that.

"Look, girl, it ain't no list…everyone gets in when I let them in. I'm running this door. So, get your ass at the back of the line or step," the bouncer announced as he looked past Dominique and Destiny like they were scum under a shoe.

"Fat fucker!" Dominique said as she took quick strides to the back of the line with her head hung low. She received a few smirks as the other girls watched her approach the long line they had all been waiting in for hours.

"Bitch thought she was special," a girl murmured to her friend.

"I am special hoe." Dominque bucked at the girl.

Destiny managed to hold her back before things got too out of hand. They weren't there to be in some brawl with random females, they were on a mission, and although it was a minor setback, the mission continued.

"I should've stayed my ass home and listened to my

momma complain than deal with this bullshit," Destiny complained as she pulled her dress down for the thousandth time that night.

"Ayeee, Dominique!" Dominique popped her head up when she heard Big L's voice from up ahead.

"There he goes bitchhh, come on. I told you." Dominique grabbed Destiny's hand. They powerwalked up the sidewalk like they were in some competition.

"Ahhhha, hating ass bitch!" Dominique licked her tongue out at the girl who'd said some smart remarks moments prior.

Big L stood a good six feet and a few inches tall. He had gold fronts that he flashed whenever he spoke, and locs that reached past his shoulders. That night he wore a black mink coat with some Levi jeans and a pair of Tims. Behind him stood his entourage of niggas who were almost as fly as him.

"You good? They ain't give you any trouble, did they?" Big L asked.

"Not too much. This Biggie Smalls want-to-be nigga almost caught the hands, treating me like a liar or some shit." Dominique looked at the bouncer with an unpleasant expression.

"I didn't know she was with you, Big L, it's not a problem at all, man," the bouncer said.

"Anyways, I have my girl with me. She's good too, right?" Dominique pulled Destiny up closer.

"Aight, they good. Let them both in and whoever else

is with them." Big L walked into the club with his entourage following closely on his heels.

"Told ya punk ass! And take them stupid as shades off nigga, ain't no sun out here," Dominque said to the bouncer.

"Hoodrat!" the bouncer replied and focused back on the line ahead.

The club was packed with mostly women like the lines outside. People were bumping into each other like they were at a jammed concert. The bar that sat at the far end of the club crowded with people ordering drinks. The music was so loud, that Destiny could barely hear herself think.

On the stage in the center of the club was a local rapper by the name of Jessica Dime. She had the crowd going live. That was one thing about the city, they did show support to their own whenever liquor and music were involved.

"Damn mane, every female in Memphis in here tonight." Destiny scanned the club. The more she surveyed the scene, the more females she saw walking around the club looking like a bitch in heat.

"It's all right, we got something they don't." Dominique sounded confident.

"And what's that exactly?" Destiny didn't see the good in any of it.

"VIP passes, bitch!" Dominique announced.

Dominique spotted Big L in the club. She headed over to him and his crew. Once they were close enough to him, he started back in his tracks down to the VIP section. He pointed Dominique and Destiny to the designated VIP area where the rest of his crew hung out.

"Y'all want some to drink?" Big L asked.

"Hell yeah," Destiny and Dominique answered in unison.

"Aight, cool." Big L signaled a waitress over to the section. "She'll take care of y'all needs. So, drink up, sit tight and enjoy." Big L dipped with his entourage he'd entered the club with, leaving Destiny and Dominique alone with a few people they weren't familiar with.

Destiny took another quick scan of the club, her shoulders slouched when her eyes didn't fall on some NBA players, all she needed was to fall in the arms of one. She'll be set for life.

"Where are all the NBA players? I thought we were going to be in their section?" Destiny said.

"We are in their section. You know how these players are extra late." Dominique put in an order for her, and Destiny since Destiny's mind was clearly not there. She ordered them shots of Tequila and Long Islands, something that was sure to make them both loosen up and mingle.

"No, I know how Memphis promoters are—big liars. I guess his name is Big L for a reason, cause ain't no damn basketball players in here." Destiny took a seat next to a heavy-set man who looked to be in his late thirties, he was busy running his mouth about the NBA game that had taken place in the city.

"Bitch, chill. This woman needs to hurry back with these drinks because you doing way too much. They ain't even let no one in, yet." Dominique took a seat beside Destiny.

They both took out their phones to snap up a few pictures, there was nothing like capturing the night and making social media females mad about a place they wished they could be.

Men draped in gold, diamonds, and expensive attire filled up the section. Some were tall, some were taller with nice athletic builds as if they owned the spot. Dominique went from chill mode to having her game face on to seduce the man of her desire. One talent she prided herself on was being able to get a man's attention and have him under her spell within minutes. Dominique saw someone she was interested in; she went in for the target. She prided herself in learning the ropes to bagging a baller. She scared a few bands along with the Land Rover she flossed around the city with her knowledge of selling rich men their dreams.

Destiny had her mind set on the task for the night. The whole night she pumped herself up about what she was going to do when a baller entered the scene. Now that the section was full, she couldn't even summon a simple, *hello.*

The thought of opening her mouth had her sick to the core.

"Excuse me ladies can I offer y'all a drink?" Destiny was zapped out of her thoughts when she heard the voice of a man. She looked at the tall man who wore simple bling than the players who were in their VIP section.

Dominique looked the man up and down like he was some shit seeping in the weeds of the lawn. She already had her eyes on a few players who were in VIP chatting away and looking rich. The man who popped up offering drinks wasn't her cup of tea. She figured since she wasn't feeling him, then Destiny wasn't either.

"Hell no! Besides, we got our own drinks and our own bottles in our own VIP with all these rich niggas," Dominique snapped.

"Damn, girl why you have to be so rude?" Destiny nudged Dominique's arm.

Dominque ignored Destiny and continued with her rudeness. "Look, I don't mean no real harm but we on a mission and it doesn't include wannabe rappers or fake ass Memphis niggas flaunting like they got bands."

The man gives a sly smirk, he took Dominique's words on the chin. He had encountered women like her before, they were after the dollar bill. He also peeped when women wanted to be the center of attention and steal their homegirl's shine.

"I'm sorry if I was rude before, so let me say that again." Dominique shifted her weight to one leg and placed her hands on her hips like she was the meanest thing that stood. "Hell, no, you can't get us a drink. Thank you, sweetie."

"Oh, it's like that, huh? You treat niggas like this who you think don't have money."

"What? You some groupie who wants to get pregnant by a rich nigga so you can live a lavish life?" The man shook his head and turned his attention straight to Destiny. "Let me try this again because I didn't have a chance to introduce myself properly."

Dominque's mouth dropped when she realized that he wasn't even paying her any mind. His focus stayed on Destiny and that rarely happened. Usually, she could hurt a nigga's feeling quickly and have them walking away with their head hung low. It didn't work on him.

"I'm Darrell Wallace Jr., people know me by DWJ or D. Wallace." D Wallace extended a hand.

"Hi, I'm Destiny Bailey." Destiny shook D. Wallace's hand.

"I know who you are. I see you in the papers doing your thang. You play for UOM, right?" D. Wallace said.

"Oh, so you a fan?" Destiny smirked.

"I wouldn't say a fan, I keep up with college ball," D. Wallace replied as he undressed Destiny with his eyes.

"We don't get as much attention as the guys. So, I didn't know too many that do." Destiny tried her best to keep it together, she was about to come undone right in front of D. Wallace.

"Well, you definitely have my attention, it's not often you see a gorgeous woman like yourself out there on the court balling." D. Wallace moved a bit closer to Destiny as if she already belonged to him.

Dominique squeezed between them like she was about to part a fight. She placed her hands in D. Wallace's face with her face balled up. "Now, I know you're full of shit because ain't no nigga really checking for no sweaty as bitch dribbling the ball across some dirty ass gym floor." Dominique folded her arms and continued to block D. Wallace from speaking to Destiny.

"Yo, you have to chill. Let me talk to the man, you don't have to be all extra. Go flirt with the niggas over there. I'm handling this over here." Destiny put Dominique in her place.

"Alright, fine, talk to the nothing ass nigga then." Dominique let Destiny have at it. She stormed away and went to flirting with a few of the players who occupied the spot.

"I'm sorry about her, she can be overprotective sometimes."

Dominque tried to control Destiny's every move. She was even trying to control whether she played basketball or not. Long as they were friends, Dominique wanted to be the one to call all the shots. Destiny allowed her to dictate everything over the years. Dominique being in charge made things simpler. Destiny didn't have to argue about who was the HBIC. Being the head bitch, meant that all plans had to be approved or denied without anyone's input except the leading woman. Destiny refused to have all of that on her plate. Dominique thought she was butter on a steak, Destiny didn't want to be the one to hurt her feelings.

"Nah, it's aight. I'm used to females like her. They can't really stand when the spotlight isn't on them." D. Wallace flashed his perfect white smile.

"Was it corny of me to mention your games?"

"No, not at all," Destiny said.

She viewed him a good second. She remembered seeing his face somewhere but couldn't place the name with the face or the location she'd seen him "You just look so familiar. Where have I seen you?"

"I play ball, too. I played for Miami. Now I'm overseas. Originally from North Memphis." D. Wallace revealed his identity. He wasn't the type to pop off or show out for a woman. He tried his best to keep a low profile wherever he decided to go.

"Oh, nice! What are you doing here?" Destiny poked around for more information.

"Supporting some of my homies. And I like to visit home occasionally," D. Wallace said.

"Oh, okay. I can dig it."

Destiny bopped to the music that played over the speaker, Jessica Dime's performance was long over, some other local rapper was on stage with his crew. The club wasn't as amped as before and the dance floor had thinned out some too.

"Look I'm not the type to hang out all night at a club, the crowd is growing thin anyway, so you trying to leave with me or what?" D. Wallace went ahead and shot his official shot. Destiny didn't give him the gold-digger vibes, that's why he picked her.

"Yeah, she can go if you have a friend for her best friend," Dominique interrupted.

Last Destiny had seen Dominique, she was in some players' faces in her own little world, then there she was again, in business that wasn't hers to be in.

"Oh, now you want to hang, huh. I was just a nothing-ass nigga earlier. The best thing for you to do is move out my face, ma." D. Wallace viewed Destiny once more. "I'll be outside if you down to ride with me tonight."

Destiny waited until D. Wallace was out of sight before she said anything to Dominique. She had almost completed her mission. The sole purpose of being there was to get in the company of a rich man and hopefully be good enough in the bed for one to want to spend some money. A part of her felt guilty for wanting D. Wallace only for what he had in the bank; however, she quickly bumped the thought because everybody had to find a way to eat in the world.

"Soooo." Desinty popped one leg in the air as if she was a princess fresh out of some Disney movie.

"I'm going to go off with D. Wallace tonight and see what he's like, and you never know, the nigga might drop me some money. I'll call you in the morning."

"That wasn't the plan." Dominique cocked her head to the side like Destiny said the stupidest words a person could summon.

"The plan was for us to get on a baller. That's what I

did, so like I said. I will be in touch in the morning." Destiny walked away from Dominique before they ended up in catfight.

"Bitch!" Dominique murmured as Destiny sashayed away.

The fact that Destiny was leaving the club rubbed Dominique in all the wrong ways. She hadn't even gotten past the greeting stage with the men in the VIP section, they were too over themselves, and they looked down on her like she was another groupie. Part of her was happy Destiny did at least leave with somebody important and not some cheap ass Memphis nigga they were used to, but still, she felt like it should've been her on D. Wallace's arm and not Destiny.

CHAPTER *Three*

Destiny walked into the hotel in amazement. The longest she'd lived in Memphis, she hadn't ever been on the upscale side. She sure as hell never stepped foot inside of any Four Seasons. The lobby was huge and spacious, not like the rundown motel she booked for her eighteenth birthday over the summer. The front desk seemed like it reached from one side of the lobby all the way to the other ends. Expensive chandlers hung from the high ceiling that appeared to cost more than the house she grew up in, possibly the entire block.

"Damn, it's tight up in here!" Destiny exclaimed.

She tried her best to keep cool. The more she surveyed the hotel lobby the more excited she'd become. Nobody ever scooped her up and took her to any fancy place.

"Yeah, it's pretty neat. It's nothing like the ones I've

stayed in overseas, they have them tight. It took me a while to get used to that way of living. Then they wait on you from head to toe; treat me like a king over there."

D. Wallace grabbed Destiny's hand in his. They walked down the hallway like they were an official couple. Destiny couldn't understand why she'd fallen for a man like D. Wallace that quick. The mission was to secure a meal ticket, yet she was there walking beside him, thinking about having an actual life with him, being some basketball wife.

"That sounds like the life," Destiny expressed.

"Yeah, you going to be living like that too, Ms. Ball Player. You already know you have the skills. You'll be in the WNBA before you know it, probably playing overseas too." D. Wallace pressed the arrow button on the elevator, a few seconds later a group of white women rushed out like they were on their own mission. D. Wallace stepped aside once the elevator was empty and extended a hand to allow Destiny to enter first.

"Yeah, maybe you right."

Destiny hadn't thought about basketball for hours, she had fixated on being D. Wallace's girl, waiting on him to come home after being away for a while, holding him down while he made the money. His mentioning of her being her own ticket out, made the fantasy vanish. The way he said it, she felt like he wasn't trying to take care of a woman like her when she had the potential to take care of herself.

"Nah, I know I'm right. You have too much talent not to make some of yourself. You like the star player at UOM.

Stop playing on your top like that." The elevator stopped on the eleventh floor, the double doors slid open, and D. Wallace allowed Destiny to exit first the way he'd let her get on.

"Yeah…I guess." Destiny pulled her phone out of her purse when it went off.

It was a message from Shirell telling her that the coach had called a last-minute practice session for the following morning. Destiny had become used to the coach pulling shit out of her hat. That night she wasn't trying to hear any of it. She was in the hotel with a true baller who could've changed her entire life with the snap of his fingers.

"What you mean? You better see your talent for what it is before it becomes what it was." D. Wallace stopped at the room that read, *presidential suite*. It was the last room on the eleventh floor.

As he opened the door, a huge glass window that overlooked the city's skyline, grasped Destiny's attention. She never received the chance to see the city that bright at night, at least not from that kind of view. She barely got out at night, usually, it was to school, then off to practice and back home. The parties she normally attended with Dominique were in the hood, house parties hosted by drug dealers and has-been musicians in cheap ass motels.

"Damn, you up like this?" Destiny strutted into the hotel room. She dropped her purse on the first chair she laid eyes on in the room. She walked over to the window and viewed the skyline. It seemed like every building in the city was lit.

"Yeah, you like that?" D. Wallace grabbed a handful of Destiny's ass, then wrapped his hand around her throat. He turned her around to him with force.

Destiny messed around with a few other men in the past, they weren't like D. Wallace they didn't take control of her the way he did.

"Hmmm," Destiny moaned.

D. Wallace raised her dress up to her hips, he ripped her underwear from her body. His hand dipped to her pussy, and he played with her clit with passion mingled with aggression. All Destiny could do was give in to D. Wallace's will over her. At the club, he was a man she was chatting with briefly then there she was getting taken over by his presence.

"Yeah, that pussy is already wet for me." D. Wallace moved Destiny's hand to his pants. She took any time to unbuckle his belt and unzip his pants to release the nice brown shaft.

"Get on your knees, I want you to suck my soul out through my dick," D. Wallace said.

Suck his dick? Destiny's mind went into overdrive. She had only gone down on a guy once. The experience hadn't been a good one either. She barely knew what she was doing, and it took the guy way too long to bust one. If she was being real with the whole thing, sucking dick frightened her in many ways. The pressure to please another person while she degraded herself sat in her stomach like undigested food. D. Wallace was only a stranger a few hours ago, but he expected her to get down and take him into her mouth.

Destiny thought of all her options. She was either going to please D. Wallace with the hope of doing a good enough job to secure a bag or leave the room with some form of dignity. The reality of her life settled into the front of her mind. Going back home meant she had to deal with another day of old food and raggedy clothes. All she had to do was please D. Wallace to find favor in his eyes, sell him the dream Dominique couched about.

"Don't be scared. Act like you know what you're doing," D. Wallace said.

Destiny dropped to her knees, she looked up at D. Wallace. Part of rapping him around her pinky meant to truly snatch his soul. She had to show out. Destiny took him into her mouth, and she went to work. She sucked on his dick as if she did it for a career. He put his hands in her hair going with the flow of her being in charge.

"Ouuu, shit. You know what you doing, huh. Shit, yeah, suck the head of that dick," D. Wallace said.

Destiny continued what she was doing, trying her best to stay focused. The more she sucked, the harder it got. It motivated her to keep going. Nothing in the world mattered more than him getting off.

"Stand up," D. Wallace demanded.

Destiny snapped herself back to reality, she harkened to his demands. She raised to her feet, he forced her to turn around and pinned her against the window. Her hands were on the glass, spread apart. He parted her legs wide enough to dip in.

"Oh shit." Destiny moaned as D. Wallace entered her with every inch he had to offer.

He thrust constantly without slack. Whenever she thought, he was going to stop, he went harder, and deeper. The act lasted so long, that she couldn't even feel her legs or her feet that were still in high heels.

"Yeah, when I'm done with you, I still want you to feel me inside." D. Wallace smacked Destiny's ass, which caused her to cry out through pleasure.

"I can't take anymore," Destiny said through tears.

"Nah, I'm not done with you. You gon' remember this dick," D. Wallace said.

He turned Destiny around and picked her up. She wrapped her legs around his waist, and he went into her again like she possessed the last pussy on earth. They went at it for another twenty minutes before D. Wallace busted all in her walls. All Destiny could do was lower herself to the nearest seat after they finished.

Destiny watched from the seat as D. Wallace made his way to the bathroom. The only way she was going to get up from the seat was if he picked her up and carried her.

Destiny woke in a fresh white shirt and some shorts that were too big for her liking. From the looks of it, D. Wallace had washed her up or at least put her in some changing clothes. For all she knew, she had done it herself and couldn't remember due to the one too many drinks she had.

"Good, you're awake." D. Wallace walked over to the bed already dressed for the day.

"What time is it?" Destiny asked.

"Eleven-thirty." D. Wallace looked down at his watch.

He glanced back up at Destiny. She was still pretty the way he remembered her at the club. He didn't get that with most women, usually, he met one who looked decent than when morning came, it looked like a completely different person he'd taken back with him. Destiny had a natural beauty that didn't come very often in the age of build-a-bitch.

"Fuck, I'm already late for practice." Destiny hurried out of the bed sore from the feet up.

"Can you give me a ride?" Destiny walked the best she could, gathering her items.

"Yeah, sure." D. Wallace agreed.

Destiny texted Shirell and told her that she would be there soon as she could. She had to pick up her car from Dominique's house and then head home to shower before heading over to the gym. It had already seemed like a task that would take a few hours. The practice would, sure enough, be over before she showed her face, the gym doors would long be closed, and her teammates would be heading out.

"I really blew it today." Destiny slid the phone back in her purse.

D. Wallace refused to read into whatever she had going on too much, he never been the type to get himself caught up in anybody's drama.

They exited the hotel without saying much of anything, Destiny's mind was all over the place, so D. Wallace decided against any small talk. He learned firsthand to allow people to have their moment. He barely knew her, wasn't much he could've said that would've made her feel better anyway.

Destiny put Dominique's address in his phone's GPS without even passing a word to him. She leaned the seat all the way back. Her body felt bruised and beat up. She hadn't processed the night she had spent with D. Wallace. With all the thoughts that raced, she wasn't sure when she would be able to ponder it.

"You straight?" D. Wallace finally asked.

"Yeah, I'm okay." Destiny lied.

"You sho?" he took his eyes off the road for a few seconds before turning his attention back to the task at hand.

"Yeah, I'm just freaking out about missing practice. I never miss any." Destiny took a long exhale before melting into the seat underneath her.

"Ahh, shit. I'm sorry for being in the way of all of that. Had I known you had to be somewhere I would've woke you sooner. I know how it is showing up late and being in the fuckin' hot seat." D. Wallace made a right turn at the intersection on the main street that led from downtown to the interstate, which lay the other side of the city, the lower communities.

"It's all right. Hell, it's my fault for fuckin' off." Destiny wanted to disappear in the seat and stay hidden until she thought it was safe to show her face to her team. Basketball was still her dream, and meeting D. Wallace had only reshaped the dream for a moment.

"Say, let me make it up to you after you get all that handled. I want to take you out tonight. I really want to kick it with you heavy while I'm still in town. Well, if that's cool with you," D. Wallace said.

"Okay, that's cool."

Destiny suddenly felt better. It gave her little hope that even if she did blow her entire career by missing one practice, she had something to fall back on, someone to catch the fall.

D. Wallace seemed to be digging her in a deep way. She was sure he wasn't going to leave her high and dry as the Memphis niggas did in the past, nor did he come off as the type who would stand her up. However, that could've come from her head being in the clouds after the night they shared.

Before Destiny could really get back comfortable around D. Wallace, he pulled his all-black Escalade into Dominique's driveway. She noticed her car being the only one parked, which meant Dominique had found her a baller too or someone better.

"Am I going to see you later, right?" D. Wallace grabbed hold of Destiny's hand before she exited the SUV.

"Of course." Destiny leaned over and gave D. Wallace a kiss.

"Aight." D. Wallace released her.

Destiny hopped out of the SUV and hurried over to her beat-up four-door car that didn't have any name of importance. D. Wallace chuckled as he watched her in a frenzy about being late. She reminded him of his younger self and how serious he took his practices. Still, he and that youth version of himself were two of the same till that day.

Destiny sat in the driver's seat; she leaned her head against the headrest as tears worked their way out of her eyes. She wanted to beat her own ass for allowing some man like D. Wallace to get in the way of things. Yet, she wanted to meet up with him again, feel him inside of him once more. Part of her knew that if it did come between choosing him or ball, she would somehow choose him. It was going to be easier that way. He already had a name for himself. Money was a sure thing. All she had to do was play her cards right as Dominique had taught her.

Basketball practice was over at least thirty minutes before Destiny arrived. She already knew where she had to go after missing a practice. Coach Davis was going to be waiting on her to show her face in the office like she saw many other players do after an absence.

"He's in his office." Shirell pat Destiny on the back on her way out of the gym.

That day practice wasn't held for the usual time, they only went over plays and a few drills. Nothing that Destiny couldn't catch up with on her own. However, an absence still was a big deal to Coach Davis.

"Fuck, here goes nothing." Destiny built up her nerves to enter the office.

Coach Davis sat behind an unorganized desk, that rested in front of two dry-erase boards with basketball floor maps on them.

"What's up coach?" Destiny greeted.

"Have a seat." Coach Davis said in an authoritative tone.

"On a day like today, you decide to skip out on practice. You have all these great opportunities lined up for you, but you choose to do heavens knows what? Destiny, you are my star player. Most of these young ladies want to be in your shoes. You have to lead by example before someone takes your spot and make you an example of what not to be as a basketball player." Coach Davis propped his feet up on the desk and rested his hands on top of his chest.

"It won't happen again," Destiny gave her word.

"I sure hope not." Coach Davis removed his feet from the desk and leaned forward with a newspaper clipping.

"First, I want to say congrats on your feature in the newspaper."

"Thanks, coach! I couldn't have done it without you. You always push me to be my best, and I promise I won't let you down." Destiny felt the energy in the room shift from being hostile to warm.

"You are welcome." Coach Davis sat up straight in the chair. He viewed Destiny with a spark in his eyes.

"Speaking of pushing you to do your best."

"What's that?" Destiny asked in anticipation.

"Those WBNA reps changed their schedule to come to see you play the next game, which is sooner than the original date they gave us. And I need you to play like your life depends on it. This here can be the start of your dream and mine." Coach Davis laid the news on Destiny.

"Oh, hell yes!" Destiny jumped up from the chair and did a move with an invisible basketball.

"I'm going to show my whole ass."

"Just play your best, Destiny." Coach Davis raised his brow.

"I will, I promise." Destiny assured.

"Now, why did you miss practice?" Coach Davis wanted to see what was happening in Destiny's life that was so important that it pulled her away from practice, he had to make sure whatever it was was under control, so it wouldn't be bound to happen again.

"Ummm." Thoughts of the night she had with D.

Wallace surfaced, and she remembered she had to hurry up and head back home to find something decent to wear since they were supposed to be meeting back up that evening.

"Oh, well, I had a friend who came in town, and I was kicking it with him. Last night turned into a crazy night." Destiny left out a few details like it being D. Wallace, who was a former player for the Heats and now played overseas, or how last night had been their first interaction.

"Him?" Coach Davis questioned.

From his years of experience nothing good ever came out of a female ball player who was caught up with some man. "Well, playtime is over. I need you to be at your best and focused."

"I got you, Coach. I'm headed to the gym right now to get some work in," Destiny said.

"You better! I have been making sure you get the exposure you need. Don't let me down." Coach Davis ended the conversation.

Destiny went out to the gym to do a few drills. The whole time she tried to focus on the next game, D. Wallace had her mind occupied. She kept replaying the time they shared and imaging the evening they were about to spend together. Having WNBA scouts watching her play had been a dream since elementary school. Now that it was finally about to happen, she failed to focus.

In the middle of her drills, her phone went off across the room, further interrupting her. She did a quick jog across the gym to answer the call and there sat Dominique's name on the screen in bold letters.

"What's up, girl?" Destiny answered.

"What's up? Bitch, you didn't even call me to tell me all the details about your night with what's his name." Dominique yelled into the phone.

"I have a lot going on right now, Dominique. Plus, your car wasn't even home when I came over there to pick up mine. I thought you'd pulled one." Destiny took a seat on the sideline bench. Suddenly the urge to do drills subsided. She needed to be back under D. Wallace.

"Girl, some players chose me and some other bitch to go chill with them. I ended up going. And I thought I was going to be chilling with this one guy that I hit it off with, but them niggas wanted a fuckin' orgy," Dominique complained.

"Did you do it?" Destiny wrinkled her face from the thought of messing around with multiple men at one time; it wasn't her type of party. It was hard enough performing for one man.

"I mean, yeah! Why wouldn't I? Plus, they broke us off some bread, so I'm good." Dominique made it seem like she had the time of her life. Dominique was known to do quite a few things; orgies weren't on the list until that night.

"Ohhh," Destiny managed to summon up a reply.

"At least you got something out of the deal, I guess. I would've dipped though. Ain't no way I would allow all of them niggas to hit, regardless of the money they offered."

"Anyways, enough about me. What happened with you last night?" Dominique pressed for information.

"I would love to tell you all the details, but I have to get done with these drills. I'll hit you up after my date with him tonight?" Destiny said.

"He taking you out? Y'all chillin' again? Bitch, I swear if you forget to hit me up tonight, I will come find you," Dominique said.

"Bye, girl." Destiny ended the call.

She viewed the basketball court for a while before forcing herself to get up and finish the drills. She finally had something to look forward to aside from Basketball.

CHAPTER Four

"Damn look at you," D. Wallace said as he viewed Destiny from the driver's side.

"Thanks, boo." Destiny hopped in the car as if being with D. Wallace was her usual routine.

Destiny spent all of thirty minutes doing drills. Before D. Wallace came in the picture, she lived and breathed the gym. Part of knowing that if she was going to be all D. Wallace's girl then there would be no turning back the hands of time.

"Yeah, you got it." D. Wallace put the gear in reverse and backed out of the narrow driveway that barely fit a normal sized car.

"If you gon' be rolling with me while I'm here then I need to make sure you looking your best. Can't have you out here in that cheap Walmart outfit. Have to get you some designer shit. Buy you some drip."

"That's cool," Destiny said.

She grabbed her phone out and sent Dominique a text to inform her that she was on her way to go shopping with D. Wallace in the city who seemed prepared to spend some bands on her. Dominique spent no time to reply, she wanted to be in the loop on every outfit Destiny received.

"What you do aside from basketball?" D. Wallace whipped the SUV onto the highway. He turned the volume up on the radio to set the vibe right. Some classic 90s Hip Hop roared from the speaker; he leaned his set further back until it was almost touching the backseat.

"Ah, I mean. I be around, not really like around. I be hanging with my girls here and there," Destiny replied.

She thought on his question a moment more, she could count on one hand what she did aside from basketball and that was hanging with Destiny or kicking it with Shirell whenever her head wasn't in the books.

"That's it, huh? Just be hanging with the girls?" D. Wallace glanced over at Destiny. "I thought you would've at least said you be at parties trying to bag a nigga. That's what you did with me, right?"

Destiny snapped her head to the side. Frowns wrinkled her forehead as she stared at him. "First of all, you approached me. I never singled you out. I hadn't looked your way."

"Oh, yeah, that's right, you were too busy in the spot trying to look good for niggas who weren't paying you any attention," D. Wallace said in a bitter tone.

They hadn't even been kicking it a full twenty-four

hours and D. Wallace had already given territorial vibes. Destiny never mind for a man to be all over her, but he was doing way too much too fucking soon from her perspective.

"Nigga get over it."

Destiny refused to follow D. Wallace up. She was focused on running up his tab in a high-end store then heading back to the hotel to give him the goodies. She figured that's why he was purchasing her clothes anyway; she'd done her job very well and he saw the need to compensate her.

"I'm already over it. I had to let you know that I caught on to the games you and your friend played back at the club. The game your friend played. I hope you're not like that. I hate to invest my energy into something that's only a come-up for you."

He'd been around long enough to know how groupies behaved. He dealt with his fair share of groupies and gold diggers, they were two and the same to him. Destiny didn't give off those vibes, he was aware of her doing her thing in college with playing basketball. So, he had in his mind that she was different, she had her own goals in life and wasn't trying to dig into his pockets and receive a come up.

D. Wallace hopped out the SUV and circled around to open Destiny's door. He never viewed himself as a gentleman; there was something about Destiny that made him want to be that way towards her.

"You open doors and shit?" Destiny said in a loud tone, which caused onlookers to turn in their direction. Her hands flew to her mouth. "I'm sorry, I ain't mean to be all loud and shit. It's, you know niggas don't do shit like that around here. You sho you from this city?"

"It's gon' be a lot more of where that comes from."

D. Wallace grabbed Destiny's hand and they headed into the Michael Kors store, it wasn't the highest priced designer, but D. Wallace peeped how women from around the way would kill over an MK bag. It was the top league for the league they were in. Besides, they weren't in too deep yet. Whenever they turned a certain point in their life together, it would go from MK to Prada.

"Ouu, I like this!" Destiny held up a blue limited edition two-toned MK bag.

"Yeah, that's fire," D. Wallace said.

He walked behind her and grabbed her waist; he pulled her closer to him so their bodies where touching. "Pick whatever the fuck you want in here."

"May I be of service?" a white sales rep walked over to Destiny and D. Wallace.

Destiny witnessed firsthand how the reps at high-end stores act whenever they thought people were there to either steal or window-shop. She visited a few high-end stores to see what they had and what the hype was all about. The whole time she was looking around she felt like all eyes were on her as if she was there to pull out a gun and hold somebody hostage.

"Yeah, I want you to go grab all the new items y'all have up in here for my girl. I'm talking shoes, handbags, sunglasses, belts, watches, you know the whole damn attire. I want her to be official." D. Wallace popped off.

"Oh." the sales rep cleared her throat.

"How will you be paying for the items today, sir?"

"All cash." D. Wallace pulled out a few bands from his coat pocket.

"Ah, sir." The sales rep said.

"Come with me, ma'am."

"Yeah, y'all do that. I'm going to be outside. I have a call to take." D. Wallace gave Destiny a kiss then he left her to shop.

Destiny picked out a few bags with shoes to match, she snagged a couple watches in all gold and diamonds and some shades she sure nobody in the hood had in their possession.

"Damn, you went all out." D. Wallace helped Destiny carry the bags across the parking lot to the car.

"I mean, you did say have fun or whatever you said. So, that's what I did." Destiny kicked her leg up like she was a princess.

"Yeah, you right." D. Wallace placed the bags in the back of the SUV, he circled around to open Destiny's door then strolled around to the driver side and hopped in.

"Aye, before we go out tonight. I need to stop by my old hood for a second, it won't take long." D. Wallace said.

"Aight that's cool," Destiny replied as she put the flashy MK watch on her left wrist.

While D. Wallace focused on getting to the other side of the city, Destiny kept snapping pictures of her watch and posting them on her social media stories. It didn't take all but a minute before her phone went to ringing and there was no one other than Dominique.

"Girl, what you want?" Destiny answered.

"I know damn well he isn't already spending money on you like that. You could've got me one if he is throwing cash."

Dominique paced through the house with her weave slipping, she was long overdue to get her hair done. The whole baller in a bag was supposed to have worked out, she had it all mapped which would've covered her hair expenses.

"Well, you know that's how a real nigga treat you when he is digging you and all." Destiny glanced over at D. Wallace with a slight smirk. If one thing was certain, he was going to spend money on her to make her see that he wasn't playing around with her like the rest of the niggas she was used to dealing with in Memphis.

"That's right." D. Wallace rested his hand on Destiny's thigh.

"Girl, stop playin', tell that nigga to spot me some money. You know how we do it. If I'm on, you on. If you're on, well bitch that means I'm supposed to be on too." Dominique took a long inhale. She sighed it out as she took a seat on the kitchen counter.

"You supposed to be my best friend, Destiny. I made sure you got in the party, the least you can do is make sure I'm straight too."

"Yeah, you know what, girl. You right. I got you,

okay?" Destiny rolled her eyes at the thought of Dominique.

The two of them weren't included when she got her new Land Rover and drove it around the city with pride while Destiny struggled to get to the next destination with her old, beat-up car. All Dominique did was get her into a party. She didn't put Destiny on D. Wallace; had Dominique run the show that night, Destiny would've never been in the position she'd landed with D. Wallace.

"You sho, Destiny? Your tone doesn't give me comfort." Dominque felt the regret creeping into her body. Maybe if Destiny would've stayed away from the party and at the gym dribbling a ball, she would've bagged D. Wallace herself.

"Yeah, girl. I'm sure. But aye I'll hit you back. I'm trying to enjoy my boo's company. You know he's not going to be in Memphis but a few weeks." Destiny looked ahead at all the traffic, she thought back to how many times she drove down the same highway with her tank on empty praying for a miracle, then there she was on the passenger side of an overseas NBA player's whip.

"Yeah, aight." Dominique went ahead and ended the call.

"Your lil friend who thought I wasn't shit?" D. Wallace chuckled.

"Yeah, she wants me to get her a few things or whatever. You know how girls be. You post one picture of what you got then they want the same shit." Destiny couldn't recognize herself by the words she spoke. She always heard about how a person changes whenever they ran into a little money, she never thought it would be her.

"She wants what?" D. Wallace said it like he was considering the idea of buying Destiny's best friend some bling. Spending money on random weren't his thing, he did enjoy popping off though. It made him feel like the man every time.

"This bling that's on my wrist." Destiny held up her wrist for D. Wallace to see.

"Oh, that shit is fire though. I mean, if you want to buy ya girl one, I'll give you the cash," D Wallace said.

"Damn. Just like that? You didn't even think about it." Destiny tested the idea.

Dominique was her girl, and she did have her back on a few things in the past, she even let Destiny crash at her house for a while when they were younger. She begged her mom to let Destiny stay with them whenever Tammy went missing for days at a time. Dominique proved herself all the time to Destiny. She was there when nobody was. Whenever Destiny needed a fresh outfit for a party, she always came through to bless her whether it was new attire or a fit she hardly wore.

Destiny admired that about her friend. Dominique showed when she wasn't obligated. She took up the slack that Tammy should've pulled. She was no one's mother, but if she was fresh when she pulled up on the scene, her girl had to be too.

"I mean, I would like for her to have some nice too," Destiny said.

"Then it's settled," D. Wallace said.

After the whole Dominique discussion, they both fell into silence and listened to the radio. D. Wallace seemed to be in deep thought while Destiny was deep in her phone replying to some replies she received from her stories. People from her college wanted to know where she purchased it from, others from her block kept asking how she was able to afford it while her fans thought she'd been drafted into the WNBA.

Time flew by that day like the speed of light. When she looked up, D. Wallace had parked and was about to exit the SUV.

"You stay put and I'll be right back." D. Wallace leaned over and kissed Destiny on the cheek.

"Okay, boo." Destiny didn't read too much into what D. Wallace had going on. He told her to stay put and that's what she was going to do.

D. Wallace grabbed a duffel bag from the back seat and headed into an old blue house that looked like it had suffered a few storms. It took him all but fifteen minutes before he hopped back into the SUV. He put the gear in drive and sped away like there was something heavy on his mind.

He drove a few miles up the road before pulling into an old shopping complex that hadn't had business in a few years. He parked around the back, so they were out of sight of anybody in passing.

"Get on top," D. Wallace said in a demanding tone.

"Okay," Destiny said without hesitation.

Destiny unbuckled her seatbelt and slipped off her shorts. She wasn't wearing any underwear, so all she had to do was cross over the seat and climb on top of D. Wallace as he had requested.

"Pull him out." D. Wallace leaned the seat back while he allowed Destiny to do her thing.

Destiny wasn't the most experienced woman he'd been with; she was younger than most he messed around with, too, so he couldn't really hold it against her. She had a few things to learn, and with his help, there wasn't a doubt in his mind that she would be good at pleasing him.

"Okay." Destiny did as D. Wallace told her. She raised up a bit to position his dick inside, then she slid down.

"Hmmm." D. Wallace grunted.

Sex had been therapy for him since high school. It was either sex or basketball. For a while it was only basketball that made him feel better. Now that basketball was more of a job, it didn't have the same effect as before. But sex had always been sex for him.

"You like this pussy, baby?" Destiny bounced up and down on D. Wallace's dick.

"Slow down for me, love." D. Wallace grabbed ahold of Destiny's hips, so she could meet the motions of his thrust. Nothing would get him off quicker than a woman who knew how to match his rhythm.

"Okay."

Destiny managed to slow down her movement, she allowed him to guide her until she got the whole thing down. She bounced a few times then slowed it down and grinded on him. She continued what until D. Wallace gripped her tighter and busted inside of her.

"Uhmm shit." D. Wallace sucked in a deep breath before he helped Destiny get off top.

"It should be some wipes in that glove compartment."

Destiny searched for the wipes without giving thought to why a grown man like him was rolling around the city with wipes. The thought did occur to her that maybe she wasn't at all special and he had a handful of other women who'd been in his whip and had gone shopping. He was in fact, a rich man and could've had whomever he pleased. Destiny bumped the thought itself because there was no way anything was going to get in the way of her being with D. Wallace. What did it matter if he had other women he fooled around with, if he'd been spending time with her and breaking her off expensive gifts?

After the whole shopping spree deal, Destiny and D. Wallace really hit it off, they went from shopping trips to her spending the night at his hotel more than a few nights out of the week. He told her up front that it wouldn't last long, because he would soon have to go back overseas to play ball..

Destiny found herself caught up to the point where she'd been missing practice more and not caring about the big game that was coming up, the one game that could've landed her a spot in the WNBA.

The end of the third week of nonstop hanging with D. Wallace, Destiny decided it was time to go sleep at home for a few nights. She'd only been home a handful of times in the three-week span, and that had been late in the wee hours while Tammy was high on her pipe.

Destiny took a deep breath as she stood in front of the raggedy door. She'd already told D. Wallace she was good, and he could go ahead and be on his way to the airport. He had been willing to put her up in a hotel for a while or wherever she felt was comfortable. Something in her soul didn't feel right with leaving Tammy all alone by her lonesome, although it probably was the best for her. Destiny did not doubt in her mind that Tammy's crack addiction would be much worse if nobody was living in the house with her. Or at least someone around to get on her ass occasionally.

Destiny clutched all the heavy bags of high-dollar merchandise as she pushed the front door open. The noise woke Tammy from her crack-induced coma.

"Where you been every day, all day?" Tammy struggled to sit upright on the sofa.

All Destiny could do was shake her head at the sight of her mother. It had been a fear of hers finding her mother laid out in the house dead. Destiny paused forward in her tracks. Tammy's voice made reality set in. D. Wallace was on his way back to the normal life that he mapped out for himself. All she had was the fancy items he'd purchased her over the three-week entanglement, along with some promises he made. He told her that all she had to do was hold him down while he was away. He would make sure she was straight. He had also encouraged her to get back focused on ball and school, but the whole WNBA dream was a dying flame since she received the taste of receiving things without having to hustle.

"Out!" Destiny rolled her eyes as she tried her best to tolerate Tammy.

"Out where? You not going to keep coming to my house anytime you feel like it. What you think this is, a hotel?" Tammy leaned forward on the couch; her sight was barely stable. She tried her best to keep her focus on Destiny, but the job itself seemed impossible.

"Been staying with some friends. It's not like you even care. Why even put on this show like you do? What you think you gon' get a pat on the back for this shit? If you cared about me, you would've checked on me." Destiny leaned against the hallway wall; she regretted not taking D. Wallace's offer of putting her up in a spot for a while until she figured out what she wanted to do.

"You make me sick, smart mouth bitch. You think you all high and mighty cause you playin' basketball and up at that lil school. You still ain't shit and will never be shit. As soon as you stop dribbling that ball, no one will give a damn about you!"

Tammy pulled a pack of Newport 100s out of her bra. She hit the pack against the palm of her hand a few times before she removed one from the pack. She placed a cigarette to her smoke-stained lips and fired it up. She viewed Destiny as she took a long, steady drag.

"And where you got all that stuff from? You better not be out there stealing."

"Whatever, Tammy." Destiny tried to keep the tears away.

Nobody's words cut as deep as Tammy's words. It could be a bitch on the street that talked down on Destiny, she wouldn't shed a tear, but whenever Tammy took a dig at her, it hit her to the core.

Destiny took quick strides into her room; she kicked the door open and slung the bags on the floor. She stalked off down the hallway back in Tammy's direction.

"Why do you always do this? Is it the drugs that get you this way, or is this just you?" Destiny wiped at the tears that rolled down her cheeks.

"I do it cause you ain't shit!" Tammy let out a breathless laugh.

"Don't nobody want your ass. Do you think everything is supposed to be handed to you because you are half white? Yo white daddy didn't even want your black ass. He left me to raise you while he went and lived his best life." Tammy hit her chest a few times as she coughed heavily.

"That's how much he cared."

"Shut up!" Destiny balled her hands into fists. She never thought of trying her mother in that kind of way, that night a bomb exploded inside of her.

"I don't even know why you wasting your time going to that school. You need to get a damn job, so you can get out of my house. You dumb and going to end up like those other lil hoes you hang 'round with." Tammy fell back on the seat as the drugs kicked in from earlier. She always overdone it because right off she couldn't feel nothing, but when they hit her system, they went on a rampage to claim her soul.

"You are old and bitter because you didn't do nothing with your life but smoke crack," Destiny fussed.

I'm not bitter." Tammy rubbed her eyes as she tried her best to take another drag from the cigarette.

"And I know 'bout the little ball player you hangin' out with. Yeah...everyone is talking 'bout it. You thought I wasn't gon' find out? The streets talk lil girl." Tammy struggled to lift her head from the couch.

"He just going to throw you away like your daddy did you."

Destiny folded her arms and stormed back off toward her room. She slammed the door and slid down to the floor as her heart fell to her stomach.

"And stop slamming doors in my damn house!" Tammy yelled.

Destiny sat on the floor crying for what seemed like hours until she decided enough was enough. It wasn't like Tammy's hurt was something new, she'd been dealing with it since she was a child, and she had in her mind that if she didn't find a way to block it all out, the hateful words would somehow shatter her soul.

Destiny fetched her phone through the pile of merchandise. Her first thought was to call up Dominique and vent, but she hadn't spoken to her in a few weeks since she'd been all wrapped up in D. Wallace. However, their friendship went back to the sandbox, which held weight, and there was no way Dominique would toss her to the side that quick. Plus, Destiny did have her gift per D. Wallace since he did agree to get Dominique something nice.

Destiny ended up calling Dominique. Shirell was the first that popped into her mind. The short time they'd been friends, Shirell showed her what it truly meant to be down with somebody. She gave the right advice to Destiny. Shirell's friendship kept Destiny's head on straight. She never boasted about it like Dominique would have.

"You up girl?" Destiny said through sniffles.

"Destiny, what the fuck?" Dominique rolled over away from the man that slept next to her with his wedding band reflecting the moonlight that shined through the poorly covered window.

"Oh, damn, don't tell me that D. Wallace done some stupid shit."

"Nah, it's my momma," Destiny sighed.

"Oh, shit girl, I thought you were talking 'bout some. Look, I'm with my man tonight. I'll hit you up later. Be easy and stop allowing Tammy to get to you." Dominique ended the call without any further words.

Destiny tossed the phone across the room! She stretched out on the floor and laid there until she eventually fell into a slumber.

CHAPTER Five

Days after D. Wallace took off, Destiny found herself slowly getting back in the groove of her old life, she even hung with Dominique a few times during the week again, and she gave her the gift that D. Wallace's money paid for. They were back going to the hood parties that were held in motels. Destiny felt like her old self, except she belonged to a true baller. Most men in the area tried to shoot their game, trying their best to show her that D. Wallace was like them, the only difference was that he made it out of the hood.

Destiny stood behind her man from miles away, she didn't allow any room for men without a reputation to steer her away from the money that D. Wallace spent on her. At every party she was fresh thanks to the shopping spree D. Wallace took on her before he left.

A few weeks in Destiny managed to catch up on the

missed practices and classes she'd skipped when D. Wallace was in the city. Now her biggest game of the season was about to happen. D. Wallace gave her some words of encouragement and told her that if she played her heart out, he would pay for her a celebration the next time he was in the city. Destiny promised that she would do her best and impress the scouts. There was nothing she wanted more than D. Wallace being proud.

Destiny stood in the locker room with her teammates and coach, they were going over a few plays before the start of the gym. The plays were centered around the way Destiny played. They had a fighting chance if the girls worked hard enough to keep the other team off of Destiny with her mean three-pointer shot that carried the team numerous of games.

"Go out there and play your best. We have some very good friends here tonight. They're expecting a great game. You will be all in tonight or off the team by tomorrow. I will not have them viewing us sideways comes the end of the game," Coach Davis said as he held a clipboard against his chest.

There was never a game the team played where they didn't see the coach worked up. When he threatened to kick someone off the team, he meant it. He told Destiny a few weeks before the game that she wouldn't dribble to see another game if she refused to make up for missed practices.

"Yes, sir!" the team said in unison.

The players started rushing out of the locker room to

head out to the floor. Destiny was one of the last ones to leave out right behind Shirell. Coach Davis grabbed her arm to stop her in her tracks.

"What's up, coach?" Destiny asked.

"I don't know exactly what you've been going through these last few weeks, but I am glad you're back in the game. Just make sure you keep it up. Don't let me down tonight," Coach Davis said.

"I gotcha coach. I told you I'm all in," Destiny gave her word.

Destiny had no choice but to be ready fore the game. D. Wallace was overseas playing his heart out, which gave her all the freedom in the world to do what she loved too. The mission to bag a rich man, gave her the inspiration she needed to keep chasing her dreams. D. Wallace had the life he wanted, and if he didn't want somebody there, he dropped them without fear of being tossed back in some hood. Destiny's WMBA drams rose back to the surface. She smelled the strong aroma of expensive wine bought by the hard earned money she made.

"Carry the team, Destiny." Coach Davis released Destiny's arm, and he followed her out of the locker room.

As Destiny walked along the hallway, the packed gym roared with fans. Her adrenaline rushed throughout her body. She even heard some fans shouting her name, or maybe she had been imagining it. Either way, she felt like a million bucks.

A packed gym always put her head in the game. Whenever she made a shot that sent the crowd crazy, she felt herself shift into another gear. She was addicted to the praise, and when her team hyped her up, it put the icing on the cake.

Now all she had to do was impress a few scouts the same way she did the crowd over the years and during her first games of the season. If she was all in, there was no way they weren't going to recruit her.

The girls gathered around the floor. The referee threw the ball in the air, and that was the start of the game. Shirell got her hands on the ball, who then passed it to one of their teammates, then the ball was passed to Destiny. Destiny dribbled the ball a few times, faked a move. She doubled-crossed a player then she shot a three-pointer the way Coach Davis told her to. The crowd went crazy, and that was all Destiny needed.

UOM won the game, they left as champions. They had sixty-points while the other team had only scored thirty-two. Destiny talked to Coach Davis after the game who had no doubt that the scouts were impressed. He told Destiny it was one of the best games she'd played, he even suggested that she go celebrate the victory.

"Girllll I didn't know you balled like that. Like I knew that's all you fuckin' do but to see you in action." Dominique hugged Destiny like she was some NBA player.

"I see all good things for you, girl. D. Wallace better step it up before you get all that shit on your own."

"Ahh, thanks girl." Destiny said.

"So, where we going tonight? I heard it's a party a few

blocks from where I stay. It's going to be nothing too crazy," Dominique said.

Any other night, Destiny would've tagged along with Dominique, but with all the extra work she'd been putting in at school and in the gym, she was drained all around. All she could think about was getting in bed and sleeping to regain the energy she burned.

"Girl I would love to go to the party."

Destiny dropped her head. She hated to let Dominique down, especially seeing her that pumped up after the game. Destiny had been trying to get her friend to come to watch her play since high school. Dominique made excuses every time. Now that she stayed and watched the whole game, Destiny felt like letting her down would put a knot in the friendship.

"I'm beat. I need my rest," Destiny said.

"Bitch, you just won a whole game. You had these people going crazy. One little party isn't going to tire you out that much more." Dominique placed her hands on her hips as disappointment wore down her facial expression. Destiny never really turned down any party. She literally tagged along for almost everything Dominique dragged her to over the years.

"You want to run a few drills in the morning before finals?" Shirell asked Destiny as she was walking out of the gym.

"Yeah, I'm down." When the words leaped out of Destiny's mouth, she instantly wanted to take them back. She'd been extra drained lately. No matter how much sleep she got, it never seemed enough. It was almost like her body was shutting down.

"Aight, I'll see you then." Shirell dapped Destiny and then continued her way.

"So, you can agree to run drills with that bitch, but you can't come to a party with me? Girl, you know what, let me know when my best friend shows up because you aren't her." Dominique waved her hand in the air and stalked off.

"Really?" Destiny shouted.

Once Dominique left the gym, Destiny found herself sitting on the sideline chairs for a long second. It was like her insides were eating itself. She couldn't even remember the last time she had something proper to eat. It was homework, studying for finals, gym, back to the gym again then the big game. She'd been living off junk food and energy drinks.

"Good game tonight girl," one of Destiny's teammates said as she walked out of the gym.

Thirty minutes after trying to talk herself into heading home, she finally found the strength to get going. She drove straight home, and time she walked into her room, she faced dived onto the bed, and went to sleep.

The sun wasn't properly up in the sky when Destiny's phone rung like an angry alarm. It was a few texts from Shirell, and when she never responded, Shirell decided to give her a call. They had early drills to run before their finals wrapped up, and their first semester of college would be behind them.

"Hello," Destiny answered.

"Get up, we got some work to put in," Shirell said.

"Aight, I'm on my way," Destiny responded and end the call.

She punched the mattress a few times before finally dragging herself out of bed. She took a quick shower, slipped on her gym clothes, then grabbed her gym bag and tossed some changing clothes inside that she could slip on after they ran their drills.

It took Destiny all of fifteen minutes to head out of the house after Shirell's call and another fifteen minutes to make it to the gym. When she entered the gym, Shirell was already hard at work.

"Catch!" Shirell yelled out.

Destiny tossed her gym bag across the floor and caught the ball like she was fresh in a game.

"Damn, you lucky I'm quick with it."

"Have to be quick." Shirell laughed.

They passed the ball a few times then they did a few laps around the gym followed by sets of twenty pushups. They repeated the drills at least twice before they dived into their stretches.

"I heard you was all booed up. You still with what you call him, the baller?" Shirell laughed.

"Yeah, girl. He sends me money and shit. I'm kind of sad he's back overseas. But he should be back in the city soon." Destiny thought of D. Wallace, her stomach fluttered from the thought of him.

"So, you actually snagged a baller?" Shirell bucked her eyes.

"Yeah, something like that. We been kicking it and enjoying each other. Well, we were before he had to go back. We be video chatting and shit though," Destiny said.

Shirell spread her legs and did a right hamstring stretch. "You sound like you really like him."

"I do! Girl, we had the best time together, and he even stayed here a little longer because of me. I guess the feelings are mutual." Destiny smiled as she thought of D. Wallace. There wasn't too many men who made her question life itself, and wasn't every day a woman fell in the arms of an overseas baller who was taller than most men alive.

"I see you cheesing hard as hell." Shirell focused on stretching her left hamstring.

"Girl I been like this since the day he took me shopping and everything. When I say he spoiled me really quick, I mean very fucking quick," Destiny said.

"Y'all had sex and shit?" Shirell threaded for more details.

"Yessss, and it was the best!" Destiny bragged.

"And you know I don't say that about everybody, nor do I let any nigga hit it."

Shirell dropped her head. She enjoyed hearing about Destiny's personal life. It was nice to see her friend happy too, even if it was thanks to some baller she only meet months ago. But she had some news she'd been meaning to tell Destiny for weeks. The time never seemed right since the semester approached the end.

"So, I have a little news too." Shirell sat on the floor with her legs crossed and her arms positioned behind her for support.

Destiny raised her eyebrow. "News?"

"I got my transfer to GSU. I'm moving to Atlanta for the coming semester," Shirell announced.

"What? You really leaving me here?" Destiny shook her head.

"You will be okay, besides you gettin' ready to go to the WNBA. That's your dream. Playing ball is just gettin' me through college, so I can get a degree. I got other plans," Shirell replied.

"Yeah, WNBA if I really impressed the scouts. But I'm going to miss you. I wish you would've given me a heads up." Destiny had to lighten up. Shirell transfer meant a bigger opportunity for her.

"You know I'll miss you too," Shirell said.

Destiny's hands flew to her right side as pain overtook her in intervals. She wanted to roll over and stay there until it subsided. Her body was already extremely exhausted, the last thing she needed was pain.

"You good?" Shirell asked.

"Yeah, a little side pain." Destiny shook it off and stood up.

"With all this damn studying and everything in between, I haven't been myself. Too much on my plate."

A few players walked into the gym, usually, Destiny and Shirell always picked the time they knew nobody else would be in the gym because they liked the private practice they received whenever they did drills together. It was fewer people, which meant they were more focused on perfecting their game without having to seem like it was competition.

"Let's run a quick game," one of the girls said.

"Aight, bet. Me and Destiny on teams," Shirell said.

"Straight, let's run it," the girl said.

Shirell helped Destiny up from the floor, running a game always brought a good time. It gave Destiny and Shirell the chance to show the other players why they were the coach's and the crowd's favorites. A day couldn't go by without someone hating and trying to take the next player's spot or thinking that if they worked twice as hard, the coach would bump them up in rank.

Shirell and Destiny got first ball. Shirell passed the ball to Destiny at the line then Destiny ran the ball across the court as she crossed a girl over who tried to hold her. She did a jump layup and fell to the floor.

Shirell and the other girls rushed over to her. Shirell slid to her knees and propped Destiny's head up. "Destiny can you hear me?" Shirell shook Destiny's head from left to right, it didn't move Destiny any.

"Call for ambulance!"

Destiny laid on the couch staring at the phone in her hand. She took a long inhale as she contemplated whether to breathe again or not. A productive morning of running drills and talking to Shirell had turned into a nightmare after she collapsed during a short game between teammates.

"Why is this so hard?" Destiny viewed the phone a moment more before she went ahead and called D. Wallace. The phone rang four times before he picked up.

"Hey baby girl, you miss me already?" D. Wallace said as he flipped through a sports magazine.

"Yes, boo. I miss you." Destiny removed herself from the couch, the same spot that Tammy usually occupied.

"Ahh, we need to talk."

"Talk about what?" D. Wallace closed the magazine and waited for whatever news Destiny had to lay on him.

"I…" Destiny trailed off, a lump forming in her throat.

"You what…you are wearing that new lingerie I had shipped to you?" D. Wallace smirked on the other side of the phone.

"Hmmm…I'm pregnant, D." Destiny's stomach tied in small knots as the news hit D. Wallace.

"Oh okay, that's what's up." D. Wallace brushed the news off like it was a joke.

"Really? Well, that's a relief. I thought you would flip out on me and make it a big deal or some shit." Destiny reoccupied the spot on the couch.

Tammy stopped in her track when she heard the news

that Destiny had dropped on D. Wallace over the phone. She eavesdropped with a smile. She did not doubt that Destiny would mess around and fuck up her life behind a man. She couldn't count on one hand the women in the family who hadn't ended up pregnant and on government assistance. It was kind of like a family curse for them.

"You didn't have to tell me that. I do appreciate it. So, I'll back off and let your baby daddy deal with all that shit. Then we can get back to us," D. Wallace said nonchalantly.

"What do you mean?" Destiny looked around with a confused expression.

He was the only man she slept with during the time she got pregnant. Before that, she really didn't mess around with anyone without protection.

"I didn't have to tell you…nigga this your baby."

"How you figure that? I can't have a child right now. And we were supposed to be having fun. It sounds like you got a situation that you need to handle," D. Wallace replied. The news itself made him ill all over.

He hadn't had a slip up like that in ages. The first and last time was back in high school before he received his big break. Back then, he was able to persuade the girl into an abortion. He lied to her like they would be together if she got rid of the baby.

"Nah, we have a situation, Darrell Wallace. I haven't dealt with anyone but you—" Destiny fussed.

"Nah, nah…you got a situation. You know the deal with being with a ballplayer, ma. So, handle your business and I will send you the funds. Plus, why fuck up your career like that? A baby will be in the way of both of our careers," D. Wallace said.

Destiny jumped up from the couch and paced the room. "I'm not killing my baby, D." Destiny moved her hands as she yelled into the phone.

"I'm not telling you to kill it. Just delete the situation." D. Wallace had it in his mind that he wasn't going to father any children. He had a career he had to focus on, and he liked the idea of having no kind of responsibilities.

"Wowww! You didn't think for two seconds about it, huh?" Destiny continued to pace the living room.

"Why do I need to think about it for more than two seconds, Destiny?" D. Wallace asked.

"You can't be serious right now. I thought you were a better person than that. Better than all these Memphis niggas who knock bitches up and take a run for it. Nah, you are two and the fuckin' same. Fuck ass nigga." Destiny's voice sounded broken.

"Hell, let's think about this." D. Wallace traced his chin with his pointer finger.

"If the baby is mine… right? What makes you think I will let my baby stay with you and your drug-addicted mom?" The corners of D. Wallace's mouth perked up.

"You have nothing, and I will prove you are unfit and take custody before you blink your eyes. So, why would you birth a child that you'll never see?"

"I can't believe you." Destiny's heart shrunk the size of a pea.

She put her trust and everything in D. Wallace. She'd invested so much of herself in him. She thought they hit it off and he would be there for her through thick and thin.

"Well, believe it." D. Wallace shook his head before he continued. "Look, I have a plane to catch. I will have my lawyer send you some cash or some to take care of that situation."

"You think it's that easy to throw me to the side, huh?" Destiny said in a rage.

"It is that easy. Destiny, just take care of it. We can act like none of it happened." D. Wallace ended the call, leaving Destiny to ponder all the words he'd said.

From the sound of his voice, Destiny felt that his words were true. He wasn't going to make things too easy for her. He gave her an option, and that was for her to get rid of the situation. Part of her wanted to get rid of the baby, but the other part knew that it would be impossible to get through the procedure without feeling guilty.

Destiny stared down at the phone in her hand in disbelief. She placed her hand free on her belly and focused on what was the right thing to do. In her heart, she didn't want to take a life. God made those kinds of decisions. Last she checked, she wasn't any God or anything close to being.

"Umhmm. I knew you would fuck your life up." Tammy startled Destiny.

Tammy popped out a cigarette and lit it. She placed it to her lips as she scrunched her eyes. "A damn baby? You know you fucked up, right? Let me guess, the nigga don't want it, huh? And now he doesn't want you. For a moment I thought you were better than me. But don't look like you not going far."

"I'm not in the mood for this." Destiny backed down from the argument.

"Eighteen years is a long, long time. Oh, yeah and you not staying here with a baby. Find somewhere else to go," Tammy said.

"Fine!" Destiny ran to her bedroom and slammed the door.

She looked at all her trophies and pictures of WNBA players and broke into a sob. She started tearing things up and throwing items across the room until she grew tired. She had life all figured out. She impressed the scouts, D. Wallace seemed like he dug her on a deeper level. It all came undone when a fetus decided to attach itself inside her uterus.

"Fuck my lifeeee!" Destiny cried until she fell asleep.

Ten months had passed since Destiny found out she was pregnant and D. Wallace blowing her off. He managed to get his lawyer to send her the money for the abortion, she sat it to the side, and more than once she thought about getting it over with and get back to the groove of things.

Instead of using the money for the sole purpose that it

was sent to for, she used it to help on items the baby would need while the job she snagged at a corner store paid for the rest. She made a deal with Tammy, so she wouldn't be out on the streets with a newborn baby.

The friendship she had with Dominique flatlined over the months. Each week Dominique came up with a better excuse to blow Destiny off. They no longer had anything in common. Destiny was preparing to be a mom while Dominique was still out in the streets trying to come up by dating a baller.

Destiny viewed DJ in the bassinet while she phoned Dominique. She chose her best friend to be the godmother to her son. She didn't even show up for the birth, which was an entire month prior.

"Hey! I was just calling. I haven't heard from you in a minute. Hell, you haven't even seen DJ yet. He's a month now," Destiny said.

"Girl, my bad, I been busy doing my thing. You know how that is…" Dominique said dryly.

"Yeah, I guess. You must get a new boo?"

Destiny longed to feel normal again. Talk about ballers with her best friend, laugh at the countless niggas she blew off on the daily and the ones who were walking around like they owned the world when they couldn't afford a pot to piss in.

Domonique smacked her lips. "Yeah, something like that. He taking care of things right. So, I been chillin' with him."

"I heard that! Girl, I'm happy for you. I wish Darrell

would come take some responsibility for DJ," Destiny expressed.

"Hell, he threatened to take him off my hand the first day I found out I was pregnant. I knew that nigga was capping. He been a no-show since."

"Didn't he tell you to get an abortion in the first place?" Dominique asked.

"What's that got to do with anything? I wasn't going to kill my baby. Besides, he is here now, and I thought he would've changed his heart. Hell, they look like twins," Destiny snapped at Dominique's rude words.

"I mean when a nigga tells you to do something, you should do whatever to hang onto the bag. But maybe he will change his mind one day." Dominque brushed off Destiny. Their problems weren't the same, and how she saw it, Destiny made her bed, so it was hers to lay in and figure out how to make.

"I got to go, girl. My new boo is taking me shopping."

"Yeah, aight. Just stop by the crib soon. I want you to meet your godson," Destiny said.

"Bye," Dominique ended the call.

Destiny tucked her phone away; she scooped DJ up and placed him in the stroller. He needed a few essentials, so while he was cooling and she had the money, she decided to go ahead and head to the corner store where she worked to pick up a few things.

"I'll be back. You need anything from the store?" Destiny yelled out to Tammy.

"Just get me a pack of cigarettes," Tammy said.

"Aight." Destiny headed out the door.

Destiny rolled DJ down the narrow sidewalk as she thought about how different things would be if she was still in school. How life would've turned out had she went to the WNBA. She tried to quickly bump the thoughts, because DJ was there now, none of it could be undone or redone.

"I'm going to figure this all out. I got us." Destiny said as she continued to push the stroller.

As she crossed the intersection, she focused on getting to the other side of the street safely. And in the process, she laid eyes on D. Wallace's SUV, the same one he drove her around in numerous times, and her eyes had to be playing tricks on her when she spotted Dominique leaned back on the passenger's side.

"What the fuck?" Destiny shouted.

D. Wallace blew the horn at her and sped off down the street. The past, present, and future flashed before her eyes. Dominique showed a lot of jealous ways over the years, she even tried to diss Destiny in front of a few boys when they were in high school, making sure the spotlight stayed away from Destiny.

Once Destiny started playing ball, she no longer had the upper hand, Destiny had fans from men to women and everything in between. Dominique took a while to adjust to Destiny being in the limelight, she had to somehow make a new name for herself other than being Destiny's good-looking friend that had the boys sniffing after her.

"You dirty bitchhh!" Destiny caused onlookers to look

in her direction. Her best friend since forever was roiling in the car with a man who'd knocked her up and left her high and dry. Then she remembered the phone conversation they had; Domonique made her feel like shit for keeping DJ.

"Mind your fuckin' business." Destiny wiped her eyes as she headed toward the store. But instead of going in turned to the block to Destiny's house as her heart drummed to the sound of her agony. Her best friend and the father of her child were happily messing around with each other, and Destiny didn't know how to live with that reality without getting some form of revenge.

Destiny walked up the cement driveway, her eyes fell on Dominique's car; it looked almost abandoned. Long as Dominique had the car, it was always kept nice and clean. Destiny figured D. Wallace was the cause of the sudden switch. She was too busy being driven around in his car to even care for hers.

Dominique pounded her fist against the door hard as she could; pain shot up to her elbow and then hit her shoulder like a train. "Hey! Mrs. Harris, it's me!"

Long steady footsteps dragged in the distance. The door swung open and revealed Mrs. Harris still in sleep-wear with crowfeet now visible underneath her eyes. Mrs. Harris wasn't some young mother like most in the city; she was old. She had Dominique when she was pushing her forties, and now old age had caught up with her.

"Well, hey Destiny. How are you and the baby?" Mrs. Harris greeted.

Destiny swallowed a lump of tears. She didn't know why she was at Mrs. Harris's front door or what revenge meant.

"We are doing just fine," Destiny said.

Mrs. Harris stepped aside with her welcoming presence. "Come on in. Dominique isn't here right now, though."

Destiny rolled her eyes, remembering the scene that made her temples throb. Dominique was booed up with her ex-lover and father of her child. Her best friend stabbed her in the back and made a joke of her pain.

"I know Mrs. Harris. I told her I would stop by and get my book from her room I left over here," Destiny replied.

"Oh Okay." Mrs. Harris took a seat on her plastic-covered couch. "Child she with some new boy. You know that daughter of mine and her love of men."

"Yes, I know all about him too well." Destiny's stomach ached. She had to think quickly on what to do to Dominique for heat-of-the-moment revenge. Any minute Dominque and D. Wallace could've rolled up and dogged her.

"She says he's some basketball player. I will be glad when she does find whatever she is looking for so she can get her life together," Mrs. Harris expressed.

"You want to hold the baby while I get my book?" Destiny said.

"Yeah, yeah, give him here," Mrs. Harris replied.

Destiny unbuckled DJ from the stroller and handed

him over to Mrs. Harris as if she was a relative then she stalked down the hallway to Dominique's room.

Destiny surveyed Dominique's room for anything that belonged to her. Since they had been friends for years, it was plenty of stuff Destiny decided to take.

"Stupid, dick-loving, bitch!" Destiny murmured.

She filled over some of Dominique's things and pulled all her clothes out of the closet and stomped them, then she walked over to the dresser and viewed a picture of them from senior prom. They looked like sisters, and in that picture, one wouldn't think that Dominque would betray her best friend. Destiny grabbed the picture as she thought about smashing it. She placed it back on the dresser and walked into Dominique's bathroom. She locked eyes with Dominique's toothbrush with amusement playing on her facial expression. She grabbed the tooth-brush and walked over to the toilet to pee. She placed the toothbrush right underneath her on the toilet and let her river flow all over it.

"Next time you won't mess over somebody," Destiny dipped the toothbrush in the toilet and scrubbed the bowl clean.

"I hope you like the taste of it." Destiny put the tooth-brush back in the cup and strolled out of the room.

"I got my stuff…off to work I go now." Destiny grabbed Dj from Mrs. Harris.

"Okay, baby. Tell your mom to call me I haven't heard from her in a while." Mrs. Harris followed Destiny to the door.

"Yes, ma'am, I will," Destiny exited the house feeling a bit better, but she knew she had to do something to get away from Memphis.

Although she did get heat-of-the-moment revenge on Dominique, there were two other options she could've chosen that day: go find Dominique and D. Wallace and beat the living hell from them or take it on the chin and boss up. She chose the latter, and she decided to get back serious about her life and find a way to stack up a little money while taking care of her son. Therefore, she dialed up Shirell with tears in her eyes and told her that she was moving to Atlanta and to make room for her and DJ.

Four Years Later

CHAPTER Six

The club was dimmed and smelled like cigarette smoke mingled with cheap whisky. Fuck Love by Young Trap ft. Too Short played over the speakers as people flooded the front of the stage to see the dancers like they did every weekend and select weekdays. Although the spot was nearly packed to compacity, the bouncers were still allowing people to come inside.

"Fellas don't be cheap…dig deep into your pockets and tip the dancers and bartenders. You know we got some of the baddest chicks in ATL. And later, we have someone special coming to the stage, one of the club's personal favorites and I'm sure yours too, so get your pockets ready!" The DJ announced over the speakers. The crowd went wild, and money was being thrown in the air like confetti.

It was one of the biggest nights of the weekend, and

Destiny had pumped herself up during the drive over, it wasn't her first rodeo, she'd been at the club a good while by then, so she the ropes were imprinted in her brain.

Destiny bumped into the club owner's girlfriend, Joseline just as she was about to enter the dressing room. Joseline was the last person Destiny wanted to see, they had some bad blood that never would come clean if Joseline refused to find a way to come down off her high horse.

"Destiny, where the hell you been girl? You on in thirty." Joseline said in her thick Spanish accent, the only thing that made the accent bearable, was her looks. Joseline had long black hair and a body most women died for. Joseline was Puerto Rican and she never failed to make it known whenever somebody tried to downplay her for another race.

Destiny viewed Joseline up and down, although she was gorgeous without a doubt, the cowgirl boots and a hat weren't the style she should've went for to Destiny.

"I know, I know, Joseline. I couldn't find a babysitter. And at last minute my friend decided to watch Dj for me," Destiny said.

Joseline balled her face up at Destiny's story; she'd heard all the sob stories over the years. All she cared about was a bitch showing up to do her set. All the problems in their life had to take a backseat, she couldn't have them out there all sad-faced while the crowd came there for a show and to spend their hard-earned money on a fantasy.

"A babysitter? Do I look like I care that you couldn't

find a babysitter? Just be ready to pop that pussy." Joseline said.

"Look, Joseline, damn, I said I was sorry, it won't happen again. I promise." Destiny swallowed her pride. She decided to let Joseline be her usual rude self, there wasn't much sense in arguing about a situation that couldn't be redone.

"You said that last time and the time before that and the time before that too." Joseline jogged Destiny's memory.

"Well, this is the last time." Destiny made her way into the dressing room with Joseline in tow.

"It will be the last time because next time you're fired," Joseline warned.

Destiny threw her hands in the air. "Joseline, I don't know why you trippin', I bring a lot of money in the club. Hell, the niggas come in this bitch to see me. I'm the hottest thing you got right now, so chill out…" Destiny said.

"My shit was lit before you got here, and the only reason you so popular is cause you fresh meat and meat spoil after a while….so, enjoy the ride while it lasts. It does get old," Joseline said as she stood behind Destiny with her arms folded.

"Your shit? I could have sworn this was Teddy's club." Destiny corrected.

"He in jail, so, I'm HBIC right now and if you don't like it, you can leave." Joseline reciprocated the disrespect.

The other dancers who were busy dressing for their sets

turned their attention in the direction of the commotion; they looked wide-eyed and amused that Destiny gave Joseline nothing short of hell. She did something that most of them were too afraid to do.

"Aight, J, damn! You know how this shit is. Chill out I'm still gettin' adjusted here with my son," Destiny replied without the attitude she had a few moments prior.

"Yeah, I do know how it is. That's why you're not fired yet…understand that this money comes before all that shit. So, get it together." Joseline structed out of the dressing room.

Destiny walked over to the chair that had her name on it. She hopped up as she tried to lighten her entire mood. She'd been trying her best over the years to provide for Dj and herself. She hadn't made the best decisions, that alone didn't take away from the trying mother she saw herself being.

When she moved out to Atlanta a few years ago, she tried to get money the legit way. She even picked up a few classes at community college, but money kept coming up short, so school had to wait again. Then one day a promoter on the streets approached her about a spot being open at Teddy's club, and she took the number down and paid the club a visit and been there since. She planned to leave the club once she got her money up and was able to afford a nice place for her and Dj.

"Don't even sweat her, ma. She gonna be out of this bitch as soon as Teddy gets out. You know what time it is." Skye viewed Destiny with her huge brown eyes, she like

Joseline was of Puerto Rican background but she was darker than most of her kind. The only way somebody could tell that she wasn't African American was when she spoke, and like everybody else, Destiny loved hearing her speak.

Destiny met Skye the first night she started at the club, she did her first set with Skye, Teddy put Skye in charge of showing the new girls how things went at the club before and after a set. Destiny and Skye hit it off since then, they hung whenever they weren't at the club dancing and called each other when a personal problem surfaced.

"Yeah, we will see. Who knows when that nigga gettin' out? The way she

running things in here he might not come back." Destiny shook her head at the thought of Joseline being in charge forever or at least until she decided to quit and do something else with her life.

"Trust that nigga going to be out soon. This isn't his first time being locked up and leaving whatever bitch he fucking at the time in charge. You know how he is. Making every bitch feel special like they going to come up and then dump them for the next. Trust... she will get replaced when he gets out." Skye been around long enough to know how Teddy picked and dropped girls.

"Yeah, you right. Fuck her!" Destiny went to applying her makeup, she didn't have to use much since she had natural beauty that most men gravitated towards, she never had to have on a full face to get attention from any man.

"Exactly, don't let her mess up your mood cause that

party we did last night was lit." Skye had to remind Destiny that the club wasn't where it all ended. They had other things they dabbled in whenever they weren't dancing at the club. The parties they attended brought them in more money than two nights at the club.

"Hell yeah. We made too much money at that bitch." Destiny smiled as she remembered the rack from the night before.

"Yo, I got another party for us tomorrow night. Some corporate clowns coming with that easy money." Skye wiggled her fingers.

"I'm down. Just got to get my babysitter on deck." Destiny never turned down an opportunity to make extra money because she knew what it felt like to not have shit to her name.

One of the new girls by the name of Drippa sashayed over to Skye. Her ass was bigger than anybody's at the club, and it was all thanks to her trip to Miami over the spring.

"Damn, Skye, you can't hook nobody else up? Where the money really at though?" Drippa said in a tone that made Skye's nerves bad.

"First of all, wasn't nobody even talking to your nosey ass," Skye snapped.

"Hell, you talkin' loud enough for the whole damn room to hear…" Drippa rolled her eyes.

Skye hopped up from her seat and got in the Drippa's face. Skye barely liked new bitches, Destiny was an exception when they first met, she didn't come off as some messy bitch.

"And once again, I wasn't talking to you. Besides, you going to pay me for hookin' you up. Remember one party I invited you to, and you didn't give me shit but made all that money? Bitch I put you on."

"Bitch you didn't even ask for shit," Drippa said.

"Bitchhh, it's the fucking code. I don't have to work for free. So, when you give me, my percentage from the last party then we will talk about the next one, other than that, mind your fucking business, puta." Skye poked the girl in her chest.

Destiny stepped between them to break up the fight that was a few seconds away from starting. "Look we all here to make money tonight. All this shit can chill until another time. It would be a mess if y'all beat each other up and be bloody and looking raggedy on stage. Nobody wants to throw money at bruised strippers."

"You right, this puta is nah worth it. Fuck it, let's make 'tis money," Skye said in her deep Spanish accent.

"Okay, then." Destiny quickly slipped into her attire for the night. She always made sure she was sparkling whenever she touched the stage, all eyes had to be on her when they decided to throw their entire paycheck at her.

Destiny heard the crowd from the dressing room getting hype because she was about to bless the stage with her presence and bad bitch essence. When Destiny first started at the club, Teddy saw that she had the body, he wasn't sure she would be able to keep a crowd entertained with her shy personality.

"Everybody calm down! Now cominggggg to the stage is one of your personal favorites, and she fine as hell too. She is one of the prettiest girls in this club. Fellas get your money out your pockets for the one and only, Treasure!" the DJ yelled into the mic.

People started to pack around the stage, Destiny had gotten used to seeing the stage crowded. Some faces had become regulars to her. They always came to throw away their hard-earned cash.

Destiny walked onto the stage in her Red Bottoms and sparkly red, revealing outfit. She wasn't the thickest to grace the stage, however, her body was top of the line without having any work done and that's what made the crowd go crazy. She had something that the other girls didn't have, she had the natural beauty which made men sink in their fantasies more.

Destiny wiped down the pole and then chalked up her hands. She grabbed onto the pole and climbed up as if she was light as a feather. Money started blowing onto the stage by the twenties, all she could see in front of her was falling bills. The sight itself made her want to go harder. She wrapped her legs around the pole and slid around it until she reached the bottom, then she slid into the American splits. That act alone sent the crowd in an uproar. Every move she performed, the more money they pulled out and tossed at her. With the way they threw cash, she figured they would be all out before the next girl was up for her set.

"Let's hear it for Treasureeeeeeee! I know y'all like what y'all see because I'm over here in heat," the Dj said over the speakers.

As Destiny continued to show out for the crowd her eyes locked on a white man that stared her down from the bar. She did a move for him, although he wasn't even throwing no money her way. Skye told her that some men with money never stepped foot next to the stage they instead watched from a distance and requested private dances.

Jackson continued to stare at Destiny as she performed her set. To people in passing, he looked like the average white man with blonde hair and blue eyes. He was someone greater than average. Jackson came with money and power. Whenever he walked into establishments, they knew his name.

"Hey, Tiff..." Jackson called out to the bartender.

"Hey, Jacks. What will it be tonight?" Tiffany asked as she strolled over to take care of Jackson's request. She knew not to make him wait too long, he wasn't a very patient man when it came down to him waiting for a drink or information.

"Give me a double of Hen," Jackson said as his stare never left Destiny.

He wanted to know her, every little detail about her. He'd been coming to Teddy's club for years, and none of the girls ever intrigued him the way Destiny did. There was something about her that made him want to know more. He saw her dance a few times, hell he was there the very first night she performed on stage, during that time his head was in a million places, however, since the clouds had lifted from over him, he was able to see the prize in front of him.

"Hey, who is that again? I think I missed the name when the DJ called it," Jackson said.

"Who?" Tiffany asked.

"The girl on stage now. I saw her a few times, but never really got her name." Jackson finally turned his attention from the stage.

"That's Treasure! She hasn't been here that long, hell, I think she started dancing like over a year ago, could be two years. I don't really keep up them like that." Tiffany sat the double of Hen on the counter.

"She is beautiful. Why is she here? She shouldn't be dancing at all. It's something about her vibe, she looks different from the rest of them." Jackson allowed his thoughts to roll off his tongue.

"Bring bottles over to my section and set that up for me…" Jackson slid Tiffany a stack. "Put this in your pocket, don't tell nobody so you don't have to share with these lazy women in here."

"Aight, I gotcha boo." Tiffany tucked the money away before Joseline or anybody else laid eyes on the money that Jackson slid.

Destiny danced harder as she saw Jackson walk to the stage, he looked at her for a long second before shooting her a wink, he tossed hundreds at her then disappeared in the crowd as if he was some random in passing. Destiny knew he was feeling her, and if she guessed his type right, he would be requesting her for a private dance or maybe something more.

"One more time for Treasureeee!" the DJ said.

Destiny went to collecting her money from over the stage, making sure not to overlook even a dollar. Money was money regardless the amount it was, sometimes a single bill went a long way during hard times.

Destiny focused on undressing out of her work attire. She liked the attention she brought her, but she despised the underwear all between her cheeks. She saluted women who liked wearing skinny underwear throughout the day because she was not built that way.

"Girl, you killed it as usual," Skye complimented.

"Thanks, boo!" Destiny slipped on a pair of jeans that complimented her figure well. Once she was dressed casually, she started at the money she'd collected while on stage. There were big bills in the mix, it was rare for a dancer to receive bills bigger than twenties.

"Damn, who dropping hundred-dollar bills on you?" Skye questioned.

"It was a white boy out there that gave me these hundreds during my set. He's definitely not one of my regulars," Destiny replied.

"Damn, girl, he must really want you. Men don't drop money like on somebody they don't want to fuck with heavy. I need to see who that papi is." Skye raised her eyebrow.

"He walked up to the stage, gave it to me and walked off. He was fine too. I wonder who he is." Destiny counted four stacks of money and secured them with rubber bands.

"I wonder if he still out there…" Skye trailed off as if a lightbulb went off in her head. Skye knew people and if she didn't know anybody, it wasn't a hard task for her to find out who they were. She was big on getting information, and for her information was easy to come.

"I don't even know—" Destiny cut off.

"Girl, let's go look." Skye grabbed Destiny by the hand and led her out the dressing room to find the man who tossed big money on the stage.

They went behind the DJ boot to get a good view of the club; it was possible to see most sections from that angle. "Over there." Destiny pointed out without trying to be obvious to be people who may have been looking in their direction.

"There he goes!"

"Oh, hell. That's Jackson." Skye said with disappointment embedded in her tone.

"Who is Jackson? I never seen him around here before," Destiny said.

"He comes in here every now and then with his celebrity friends. I don't know what he does exactly, but he is known around town and has a nice whip. He doesn't pay for shit or get a dance, so him throwing money saying a lot of things." Skye dropped all the tea on Destiny.

"He cute but I wonder what those pockets really look like. I'm not trying to mess around with no average ass man." Destiny sucked her teeth.

"Those pockets are fat. He normally doesn't even walk to the stage to tip a bitch. I think you hooked."

Destiny headed back to the dressing room with Skye in tow. She had to finished gathering her belongings before she left the club for the night. She knew how much the dancers stole each other items, and she didn't have time putting a heel in someone's forehead for trying her.

Destiny sat in the chair and removed the makeup from her face. One thing Skye made sure she embedded in her was removing the makeup before leaving the club because wearing the makeup home after a long night was hard on the skin.

"Are you doing this party tonight that my homegirl invited me to. Plenty of tricks with money going to be there." Skye refreshed her full face after she removed the makeup she wore during her set.

"Dj with the babysitter and she is expecting me to come pick him up at the time I gave her." Destiny pulled her hair up into a neat ponytail.

"Look, you know this money don't stop and you tryin' to roll with the big dogs. Besides, don't you and your home girl stay together?" Skye applied a thin layer of red lipstick.

"She'll be fine."

"Yeah, you right. I could use some extra money, even though they spent more than usual tonight and that white dude tossed them hundreds, I need some real bands." Destiny hopped up from the chair and laced up her Jordan's retros.

"Shid, let's go."

"Yes, bitch! That's how you make it to the top." Skye said.

They fell into the laughter as the other girls looked in their direction. The side jobs they had aside from dancing at the club was their business and they didn't' have to pay anybody a cut from their hard-earned profits, pure profit without a middle man.

Destiny crept into the house as she prayed Shirell was somewhere in bed by then. She fell short on her word another weekend; she had made a promise that after her set she would be on her way home to pick up Dj so Shirell could be free to do whatever.

Destiny passed by the living room and spotted Shirell sitting on the couch watching tv like an angry mother from the sixties.

"Oh, hey Shirell," Destiny greeted.

"Thanks for watching him again on short notice." Destiny said the words lightly. All Shirell could do was pause the tv to get a good look at her friend.

"Short notice? Hell, you didn't come home, D. You can't keep doing this, you need to get yourself together and be more stable for your son. Your son!" Shirell hadn't ever raised her voice at Destiny but that morning something went through her and pushed right to the edge.

"Stable? What do you mean by stable?" Destiny questioned.

"Stable. Did I stutter?" Shirell fussed.

"I am stable. I'm here ain't I? I work my ass off; I give you money and help pay bills around here. It's not like I'm sitting on my ass and somebody is taking care of me. Dj don't want for shit in life because I go out there and make it happen," Destiny said.

"Your son barely sees you, you always gone either dancing or with some trick. Hell, when you're not doing that, you are partying your life away." Shirell raised her phone up for Destiny.

"Do you see what time it is?"

"I was working. I do what I got to do to pay bills and take care of my son. I provide food and clothes for him." Destiny folded her arms as she thought back on the night. The night was all work and no play, she had to shake her ass all night to rack up, and dancing took a lot of energy and sometimes she took substances to give her the courage.

"Skye had an extra gig for me, I took her up on the offer."

"Yeah, you provide the material things for him. What about being a mom and being a responsible parent to him?" Shirell stood behind her side of the argument; she was the one who was there for Dj whenever he needed an actual parent in his life. When she agreed years back to let Destiny come stay with her, she thought it was would for the best Destiny and Dj since Memphis wasn't a good city to really raise a child.

"Whatever. I don't need you judging me. I just need you to keep him sometimes. It's not like I don't pay you and have the bills in here." Destiny defended her case.

In her eyes she was doing all she could as a parent. She'd been putting on for Dj since before he came into the world. It had always been her going out her way for him, and now that he was growing older, there were certain sacrifices she had to make.

"I don't care about the little change you give me. I care about Dj and I care about you. Atlanta is a way faster city than Memphis and you can really get caught up in trouble here. You can't keep going down this road." Shirell tried her best to get through to Destiny. It would've consumed her if she one day received a phone call that Destiny was dead or if she somehow went missing.

Destiny took a seat on the couch, after a long night of dancing and small talk, she could barely feel her body. Reality itself felt like a hazy dream. Normally she could get home and go crash without hearing Shirell complain. The longest she'd live there, Shirell seemed to understand that she was trying to make a way the best she knew how.

"Shirell, everyone can't be like you with your corporate job. You are smart and always been smart even in college and I'm sure before that too."

Destiny leaned back on the couch and closed her eyes. "What happened to Atlanta being the place to be—all that black people coming up out here bullshit? Now you telling me to be careful like I'm fucking around in the hoods of California."

"Destiny, you are smart too. We went to the same for a while college." Shirell shook her head.

"Remember?"

Shirell removed herself from the couch, she'd had enough of Destiny for one day. It's not like nothing she said was getting through to her. With everything she said, Destiny had a comeback.

"All I had was my hoop dreams. Having Dj kind of ruined that shit. I tried to find a job when I got here but it didn't work out. But look, I'm making way more money than I could've ever imagined," Destiny said.

"You better than this shit. You better than the chicks you hang out with. Go back to school to finish your education, D." Shirell grabbed her items off the end table and headed out of the living room.

"I'm not going to be doing this long. So, chill. I got tim—" Destiny cut off when an alert went off on her phone. It was a text from Joseline informing her what time her set was for the night and not to be late because her ass was hanging on the line.

"Whatever your son is in the room," Shirell said.

"Ayeee!" Destiny jumped up from the couch and ran after Shirell before she could get out of the front door. "Can you do me a favor and watch Dj again tonight? I have a set to do tonight but I promise I'll be home right after."

"Sure Destiny! Anything else you need from me?" Shirell said sarcastically.

"Nope that will be all." Destiny grabbed Shirell and embraced her.

"Well, great then. Just splendid." Shirell kept up her sarcasm.

"Oh, yeah, I forgot, Dj have a parent-teacher notice in his bag. So, you might need to check on that," Shirell said.

"Shit! I don't have time to talk to no damn teacher." Destiny barely remembered the last time she was in a teacher's face about Dj, she made a million excuses whenever they wanted to talk to her and eventually, they either forgot about her needing to see them altogether, or Shirell grew tired and went out there and pretended to be his mother.

"Maybe you should. Maybe it'll help your son…for once." Shirell rolled her eyes at Destiny's inability to be a proper mom.

"Why you so serious now? We used to have fun and hang out especially when I first moved here. You're so fucking boring and extra now." Destiny complained.

"Yeah, I did all of that to show you a good time when you first got here but you know, Destiny, some people grow the fuck up. We not in college anymore, this is the real world. You should really think about it." Shirell headed out the door before she had to put a beating on Destiny for being disrespectful when all she was trying to do was help her see that she was neglecting her son.

"Think about what?" Destiny yelled out behind Shirell.

"Growing the hell up, you might like it." Shirell got in her car and pulled off.

"Fucking bitch!" Destiny stomped away from the door.

CHAPTER *Seven*

Destiny focused on dressing before the dressing room was filled to compacity. She made sure she arrived long before it was time for her set because last night Joseline didn't play no games. While Teddy was locked away, Joseline was determined to keep business running while at the same time aiming to make the club earn more than when Teddy was running things. It was her way of showing him that he could depend on her without being worried.

"Hey, boo!" Tiffany walked into the dressing room. Tiffany bartended at the club, and when she could she did a few sets on non-popular nights to get her feet wet in case she wanted to become a fulltime dancer at the club.

"What's up?" Destiny greeted.

"I got someone that's interested in you." Tiffany took a seat in Skye's chair.

"What? He wants me to come out and dance for him? Just give me a minute." Destiny removed her hair from the ponytail and allowed her inches of high dollar Brazilian hair to hang. Anybody who were into hair and looking nice, knew that it costed at least an arm and leg to get the kind of hair that Destiny rocked. She liked to keep her hair black and wavy, but it had to have length.

"Umm, something like that," Tiffany removed herself from the seat. She viewed Destiny in the mirror, she never really messed around with women, but for Destiny she would've been the spaghetti that got wet and bent.

"Something like that? I'm not doing anything else. Wrong chick for that, Tiff." Destiny had to make it clear about her limits and boundaries. She saw the girls got hot and dropped it on a dick for a little bit of money, she had morals if not anything else.

"He's not that type of customer, bitch. He will be good to you. Trust me, if you believe anyone in this club who will it be?" Tiffany ran her hands through Destiny's hair in a seductive way.

"You of course. You know everything." Destiny smirked at Tiffany.

"Then go talk to him and see what's up," Tiffany said.

Destiny let out a light laugh. "You know how I get down. Money talks. Bullshit walks." Destiny combed through her wig.

"Well, he asked for you and he never do that, so, come out here and see what it's about. Like I said, he's not the one you want to ignore," Tiffany replied.

"I'll be out in a sec," Destiny said.

Tiffany turned away and headed out the dressing room. "It's stank in here, y'all hoes need to spray."

"It's probably your top lip," Drippa said.

"Shut up before I bust yo lip." Tiffany bucked at Drippa and headed on out the door. It was her enjoyment to make the dancers mad whenever she popped up in their dressing room. The only dancers she really liked was Destiny and Skye, all the other girls tried too damn hard for her liking.

Once Destiny finished up with dressing, she walked out into the main lobby in search of Jackson. She viewed Tiffany from where she stood. Tiffany looked at her and nodded from the bar area in the direction where Jackson sat.

Destiny bent the corner and headed in Jackson's direction. He sat in one of the VIP sections surrounded by a bunch of black men throwing money at dancers. Destiny walked up in the section like the baddest woman walking and to many men that met her, she nothing less than that.

"Where's Jackson?" Destiny asked.

"Oh, that's me." Jackson flashed his perfect white teeth at her.

From the looks of it, he wasn't the typical white man that hung around black men and tried to fit in, he had his own things going and the way he talked, people would've thought he was come corporate man.

"I heard you was looking for me?" Destiny pulled her

blunt from her bra and fired it up. She took a long drag and blew the smoke in Jackson's face.

"You heard right, you caught my eye," Jackson said.

"I have that effect on people, so what else is new?" Destiny charged the smoke to hear lungs that time around, she coughed a few times before she regained control.

"I'm not most people." Jackson corrected.

"Then who are you because I certainly don't know you." Destiny took another puff from the blunt before putting it out.

"Fiesty, I like that but where are my manners. I'm Jackson and you are?" Jackson formally introduced himself.

"I'm Treasure and you are Jackson who? Is there a last name, Jackson?" Destiny rolled her eyes at how little information he gave her. Niggas who wanted to have her spilled their hearts out without her having to ask them to offer.

"No, ma'am, the first name speaks for itself." Jackson got a good look at Destiny, he knew she was bad from watching her dance the night before, but she looked better up close and personal.

"I wasn't asking you for your stripper name. What is your real name?"

Destiny shifted all her weight to one leg. "Only the people who know me calls me by my real name."

"Well, I'm trying to be one of the people that'll make you forget you even worked here. I mean, if you give me a chance." Jackson placed his offer on the table without hesitation.

"It's Destiny! No last name. So, let's stop the small talk

and you tell me how I can help you because the money you threw at me last night tells me you want more than a conversation." Destiny wanted to get straight to the real point. He was doing all that smooth talking but that wasn't cutting it for her. She wanted to see what he was about.

"I can help you more than you can help me," Jackson said.

"Of course, you can, I heard this before." Destiny turned away from Jackson.

Jackson grabbed Destiny's arm to prevent her from walking away. "I honestly think you are the prettiest girl in this club. I don't know why you here."

"Because I have bills to pay and a son." Destiny snatched her arm away from Jackson.

"What are you looking for?" Jackson asked.

"What do you mean exactly? I know I'm not looking for a man." Destiny continued to with the attitude.

"And no one said I'm looking for a woman." Jackson furled his brow then fixed his eyes on Destiny.

"Most girls here are looking for money and a purse. Thar's all they seem to want out of life…"

"Money first, some fame doesn't hurt. I had dreams before this." Destiny suddenly felt like she could drop the snappy persona. She had to find her manners and give Jackson the benefit of the doubt. Tiffany said he was worth the conversation, and Tiffany hadn't ever led her wrong.

"Check this out, I'm well connected, I can get you in some videos for starters," Jackson replied.

Destiny's mouth nearly fell to the floor when the words

hit her. "Videos? I'm not doing no porn. I don't want to be that damn famous, every nigga and their patna jerking off to my pussy."

Jackson let out a slight chuckle. He cleared his throat and regained his professional approach. "Oh no, you must have misread things. I'm talking music videos. I have a lot of celebrity friends." Jackson snapped his fingers at his friend, Zane who sat in the section getting a lap dance.

"Yo, Zane, I want her in your next video, man." Jackson pointed to Destiny.

Zane lowered his sunglasses and viewed Destiny a minute before he gave an answer. "Sure, whatever you want…she def is fine as fuck."

Jackson turned back to Destiny. "See you got your first big video shoot already…"

"You are a manager?" Destiny questioned.

"No, but if you want me to be your manager I can be."

"You still haven't told me what the hell you do," Destiny said.

Jackson grabbed ahold of Destiny's hand and led her to a nearby seat within the section. Destiny took a seat and crossed her legs; she was fresh in her set attire. The other dancers who were hired for their private section were side eying Destiny because they wanted the spotlight only on them. Destiny seemed to always pop up whenever men were throwing big money. She usually bagged all the money for herself without offering anybody a cut except Skye.

"I'm someone you need to know and someone that can

help you get out of this club. Take my number and give me a call. We can set up a meeting at my office or anywhere besides here. I can show you what I can do." Jackson further laid the offer on the table.

Destiny handed Jackson her phone to input his number. He took it without hesitation, it took him all but three seconds to lock the number in. he handed it back to Destiny and she tucked it away.

"Jackson! How is my favorite person? Are you being properly entertained by Treasure?" Joseline stopped in her tracks when she laid eyes on Destiny near Jackson.

"What's up Joseline, and yes she is a perfect fit for me," Jackson said.

As they were chatting it up the waitress who were attending to their section walked up and handed Jackson his tab. Joseline instantly snatched the tab back up. "Oh no, sweetie, you know the rules. Jackson doesn't pay here."

"Oh, I forgot," the waitress said.

"I'm going to help you remember. Charging you extra for being stupid. Now get!" Joseline fussed. Joseline faced palmed herself.

"Sorry, another new girl."

"When is Teddy getting out?" Jackson asked.

"Soon, I hope. I'm tired of these hoes in here. I'm ready to get back to just being his girl," Joseline said.

"Good. Let him know business is still going as usual," Jackson replied.

Joseline looked over at Destiny. "I need you on stage,

next, you haven't danced since you clocked in. I'm charging you extra tonight for being lazy."

"Are you serious? It's already slow in here tonight, you going to make me go in the negative," Destiny complained.

"Now, Joseline, that's not necessary. She's been a great host to me and I'm sure that covers what she would have made up there tonight, right?" Jackson chimed in.

Joseline gave a weak smile. "Of course."

"Good. You can go now. I'm still talking to her." Jackson shooed Joseline away, so he could finish chopping it up with Destiny.

"Damn! You must be somebody to shut her ass up like that and no tab. Okay, I see you handsome," Destiny said in a playful tone.

"Like I said, I'm someone you need to know. I have to get going, give me a call later and we'll talk more." Jackson exited the section with his boys in tow. Destiny sashayed over to him before he got out of sight.

"Oh, yeah, I like diamonds so miss me with those bags." Destiny had to let it be known she couldn't be bought with high end merchandise the way D. Wallace done her years back. She was young and dumb then and failed to know her worth. She wasn't some hot-in-the-ass teenager anymore. She sure didn't find the bragging rights in a purse and watch how she used to. With growth came with the need for bigger things.

Before Joseline was able to hunt her down, Destiny went ahead and told the DJ to play her track. Although she had Jackson in her back pocket, she still had to put on a show for the men who were there to see her.

"Coming to the stage...Is our favorite girl. Treasureeee!" the DJ announced.

Slow Motion by Trey Songz blasted from the speakers. The small crowd gathered around the stage, some ballers and some regular men who were there to spend their paychecks. Destiny wiped the pole. She went up and down like pulling on a man's shaft. Then she tossed the rag to the side and slung her hips with the drop of the beat. She rolled on the pole and dropped into the splits and made her ass cheeks bounce one at a time. The crowd went crazy. They tossed money at her by the tens and twenties. She was somehow having a better night than the night before although it wasn't as packed.

As Destiny entertained the crowd, her mind fell on Dj. Shirell had been right after she thought it over for a moment, he was getting older, and he needed her there more now for values to be instilled. It was bad enough that a father figure was nonexistent for him. And on the motherly side, Shirell tried her best to be there for him and answer all those childish questions that were essential for this growth.

Destiny scooped up her money and exited the stage, she promised Shirell that she would be back on time that night and of all days, she wanted to make sure she was a woman of her word. Shirell had been pulling a lot of slack, and Destiny of all people made sure to acknowledge it.

"Girl, you want to have a few drinks after my set?" Drippa asked.

Destiny slung her duffel bag over her left shoulder, usually she would take anybody up on any offer of drinks after a long night of entertaining the crowd.

Destiny shook her head. "Nah, I'm good on it tonight. I have some things that needs my tending to."

"Okay, boo, I'll be seeing you," Drippa said.

"Fo sho." Destiny headed to the back office to give Joseline her cut of the earnings.

When Destiny first stated it was hard to understand why she had to split money with anybody when she did all the work on stage, nobody else was up there with her having to keep niggas entertained.

Joseline sat behind the desk on the phone with her feet propped. She glanced over at Destiny and rolled her eyes, Joseline liked competition. It wasn't a competition with Destiny; Destiny took the icing off the cake. They already wanted nights highlighting her in the club. Men wanted to pay extra to see her dance. Joseline looked good and had the crowd going crazy when she used to do sets, now she was fading away like old news.

"Hold on really quick. I have to take care of something." Joseline placed the phone face down on the desk. She removed her feet from the desk and sat up straight in the chair.

"How did it go out there?"

"It was straight. I think I had a better night tonight

with the small crowd than with the big crowd from last night."

"Hmm, well that's a first." Joseline ran her hands through her long, black hair.

Destiny was it, and even she couldn't deny the truth. As much as she wanted to dislike Destiny, something stood out and forced her to like her. "I saw you being all close in personal with Jackson. If I was you, I wouldn't get my hopes up too high. I'm saying you're not the first girl he done snatched up from some club, just know you won't be the last."

"I'm not worried about any of that. It's all a money thing for me, baby. I do my own thing my own way, a nigga is a plus when it comes to money." Destiny sat the duffel bag on the desk, Joseline flipped it over to pour the money out.

"Yeah, that's what every bitch says before the right man get in their head. You have to understand one thing, it's always money before a man, no matter how good they speak or what they put you on to. I'm speaking from experience and not what I've been told." Joseline placed the money on the counting machine, the machine accepted the money and shot it back out quicker than it went in.

"Four bands in a night. That's not bad at all. But you already know what it is, I take fifty percent off the top," Joseline said.

"Fifty percent? What the fuck happened to twenty-five? You must be smoking a fat ass dick. Teddy never charged me no fifty percent, not since the whole new shit wore off," Destiny complained.

"Teddy isn't here is he?" Joseline said.

"You know what I can find someplace else to dance. I don't need this shit. You always giving me a hard time and talking that negative shit. You don't want me here, then I don't fucking have to be here. Find a stupid bitch to fill my spot with." Destiny grabbed her cut of the earnings and turned to leave.

"Hold on, you know what. We can stick with the twenty-five percent, even though I don't really like you, I know I can't afford to lose you right now over some weak percentage." Joseline slid Destiny over the rest of the money. "Here, now go sleep your attitude off." Joseline tucked the money away and grabbed the phone.

"Yeah, I'm back. Hell, yeah. I'm sick of these weak bitches."

"Bitch whatever!" Destiny shook her head and headed out.

The crowd she pulled into the club was going to follow her wherever she chose, so finding another club wasn't a worry. A few owners were trying to get her from Teddy since day one. All she had to do was make a phone call and be done with it.

CHAPTER *Eight*

Shirell and Dj occupied the couch watching scary movies when Destiny made it home after midnight. On a simple night, he would've been tucked away for the night. Shirell never played around with Dj's bedtime, but since he'd done good in school and received great grades, she figured he deserved a reward.

"I didn't think you would be back so soon." Shirell paused the movie.

Dj jumped off the couch and ran to Destiny. He hugged her as he seemed to melt into her.

"What you got in those bags, momma?" Dj reached for the bags.

"I grabbed some Chinese food and a bottle of Don Melchor." Destiny smiled at Shirell.

"It is one of your favorites. It's really the least I can do, and who would've thought you two were having a movie night. Nothing like good food and a good movie." Destiny pat Dj on the back before walking into the living room. She sat the food on the end table and plopped onto the couch next to Shirell.

"Food isn't going to make things right," Shirell said.

"I'm trying okay, I really am trying. I told you, I would be back on time to get Dj and look I'm here, right?" Destiny raised her hands in the air and slapped them against her legs.

"I guess I can't be mad if you bought food and Don Melchor." Shirell draped her arm over Destiny's shoulder. "I know you're going to get it together."

"Yeah, I really hope that's the case." Destiny removed the food from the bags and placed the boxes on the table.

When she first moved out to Atlanta, Shirell bragged on the ghetto Chinese food she picked up on Fridays from a Chinese restaurant that sat directly in the heart of the hood, she claimed they had the best food. It had come tradition to her. She put Destiny on, and they would have nice adult beverages on Fridays along with Chinese food, then kicked back after a long week. Destiny was still trying to find a decent job, while Shirell worked her ass off for a promotion at hers. Fridays used to make them see hope in their hard work.

"How was it tonight?" Shirell never asked about Destiny's involvement with being a dancer, there wasn't a doubt in her mind that Destiny was better than shaking her ass for others' pleasure.

Destiny let her dreams die long ago to take care of Dj, but she still had the potential to redirect her future.

"It was good, made four racks on one set. And the crowd wasn't as big." Destiny handed Dj his eggrolls, he wouldn't eat anything else from the restaurant except eggrolls, she made sure to get him two helpings in case he wanted more when the morning arrived.

"Damn! I know you make money. Four racks in one damn night and for one fucking dance? Girl that's crazy, I knew people spent money on crazy shit, but they really drop money like that?" Shirell steered clear of asking Destiny about her earnings; long as the bills were being paid equally the between information was irrelevant.

"I mean, it's not like that all the time, that's why I be doing extra gigs on the side. I believe that I landed on the right path last night though. This white dude wants me to be in videos, he wants to manage me," Destiny said.

Shirell stuffed her mouth with roasted pork Lo Mein, she pressed play on the movie for Dj. It wasn't her first time seeing Halloween, so it didn't matter if she missed a scene while talking to Destiny.

"You have to be careful with these ATL managers though, not all of them are legit. You should do your research on him before you even work with him or get involved. Like what makes him so qualified to manage someone?"

Destiny removed herself from the couch to fetch two wine glasses and a corkscrew. Whenever she had a conversation with Shirell a strong drink was mandatory. Shirell didn't mind telling Destiny what she needed to hear and not what she wanted. Everybody else enabled Destiny's behavior and couldn't care less if she got used and ran over on the streets. She wasn't their responsibility in the slightest way. That was the difference between Shirell and Skye, Shirell was an actual friend who wanted her to go down the right path while Skye moved out the way and allowed Destiny to make choices whether they good or bad.

"The girls at the club says he's good, he doesn't give this opportunity to many people. And from what I know he's friends with a lot of celebrities out here." Destiny sat the glasses on the table. She opened the bottle of wine and poured Shirell a glass first before pouring one for herself.

"Still, you need to find him out for yourself. Don't go on what someone tells you. People don't give a damn about others for real. You have to look out for yourself, Destiny. That's always been your problem, you trust people before they show you whether they are trustworthy or not. If you don't put a handle on that shit now, it will be your downfall later." Shirell took a sip from her glass.

Destiny ate two spoons of food before she summoned up a reply to Shirell. All she wanted was a friend, she didn't want someone always telling her what to watch out for or how to live her life. She craved the old Shirell, the one she met back in Memphis, the college Shirell who allowed her to be who she was without casting judgement.

"You know, Shirell, maybe that's your problem. You never let anyone in. You don't trust people. You always thinking someone is out to get you. Loosen up a bit, you never really had fun back then and you acting all downish now," Destiny replied.

"Destiny, when are you going to learn that a hard head, lands you right on your ass. You should know that by now." Shirell turned her attention back to the TV.

"How about you be a friend and leave it there? I don't need you acting in the place of my momma." Destiny hopped up from the couch.

"D, take a seat and chill. You don't have to run for the hills whenever I say something you don't like. Dj haven't seen you all day. I'm sure he would love to watch a movie with his momma." Shirell finished up with her food and capped off the first glass of wine, and poured a second

"Fine." Destiny brushed the conversation off. Once again, she knew Shirell was right, however, her ego made her take the advice and place it in the dark.

With all the hostilities aside, they bonded over the movies. For the first time in a long time, Destiny felt like she had her best friend back and not the person who slowly tried to become a motherly figure in her life.

Dj basked in the time that Destiny spent with him and right before the first movie ended, he fell asleep between her and Shirell, leaving the two of them with basic passing of words about the movie. But Nothing mattered that night, the past nor the future.

Destiny made it her task to take Dj to school and give Shirell a real break away from a child that wasn't even hers to be stressing about. Shirell took the news lightly, she didn't question Destiny's sudden interest in wanting to be involved, she sure as hell didn't take credit for waking her up to reality. Destiny also made it her priority to talk with the teacher since she missed the last parent-teacher conference.

"I'm happy you decided to have a word with me, Destiny. I wish you would've made the conference the other day." Gale walked along the hallway with Destiny in tow. Since the conversation had to happen, Gale asked another teacher to watch over her class until she finished her discussion with Destiny.

"I know being a young single mother isn't easy. Being a mother, itself is challenging. Yet we still must try our best to make sure our children are properly taken care of and is receiving the best of treatment for their advancement in the world." Gale stopped in her tracks and looked over at Destiny.

She encountered all kinds of mothers from different walks of life. Many had a sob story, but they tried their best to do right by their children, even if that meant putting themselves and their lives on the back burner.

"Where is conversation going?" Destiny questioned.

Gale tucked her gray hair behind her ear. "Shirell, I believe she's your friend. She's been the one dropping Dj off and picking him up, showing up and pretending to be his mother whenever I call. She's looking out for him, and I thank her because at least he has someone in his corner. But Destiny, you are his mother, you need to step up. Dj has been excelling in school, but he's not one hundred percent involved all the time, some days he seems disconnected and out of sorts in the world." Gale looked at Shirell underneath her glasses.

"I don't know your lifestyle and I won't pretend to know. But make sure you think about your son. He needs you more than anybody."

"So, that's why you needed to see me?" Destiny placed her hands on her hips and shifted her weight to one leg.

"Ma'am, with all due respect, who brings my son to school and pick him up is my damn business. Shirell is like family; she looks after him when I can't. I bust my ass out there to make a living for my son and for you to sit up here and judge me is bullshit. Children have their ups and downs like adults, it's called being a fucking human."

"Destiny, I didn't mean to offend you. It's my job to look out for my students. I would hate for CPS to be involved when something like this can be corrected," Gale said calmly.

"Is that a fucking threat?" Destiny snapped at Gale.

"You know what, my son doesn't have to go to this stupid ass school, I'll find a place that's understanding of a single mother. Your old ass sitting up here, threatening me because my son has a few bad days."

"I'm not threatening you in the slightest way, I'm simply telling you that Dj is having some problems in school. If you can't see it for yourself then maybe you should take a look in the mirror to see what's causing it." Gale fixed her eyes on Destiny for a long second.

"I used to be like you, all hot headed. I thought I had the world all figured out. I hated listening to advice because nobody understood my pain and struggles. Sometimes you have to listen." Gale turned away from Destiny and walked back down the hallway to her classroom.

"Have a nice day, Destiny."

Destiny leaned against the wall with her mind in a million places, she had been trying to give Dj the best life since before he was born. She worked at all the shitty jobs to put food on the table without shedding a tear. She failed to understand why nobody saw that she was trying her best to make sure he was taken care. He had clothes on this back, food on the table, he had the latest technology that most children twice his age were begging their parents to get. It wasn't like he stayed in trap houses and wondered the streets while she was in the streets.

"Fuck these uptight ass people." Destiny finally found the strength to move herself from the wall and head out of the school.

Destiny and Skye sat on the patio of Maria's Mexican Grill, an upscale restaurant near downtown Atlanta. A lot of businesspeople and people who were somebody dined at the restaurant, the food was top tier, and the service was nothing less. Thirty minutes and three drinks into them enjoying the environment, Britney sashayed in. Britney was a prissy hood chick who got around with all crowds, she knew everyone there was to know in the city. However, she kept a low profile.

"Oh, chile, that hot lanta traffic not playing today." Britney took a seat beside Skye.

"Bitch, it took you long enough to get here. We started drinking without you," Skye said as she capped off her Boulevardier. Skye liked upscale drinks the same as she liked food. She came from the heart of the hood, but she'd had her fair share of rich men who changed her taste in things completely.

"Girl, even if I was only five minutes late, you were going to start drinking without me with your drunk ass." Britney giggled.

Yeah, yeah, you right, bitch." Skye laughed.

"Brit, where the hell you been? We haven't seen you at work in forever?" Destiny asked.

"I'm not going back to work until Teddy gets out of jail, and back runnin' the club." Britney looked over the drink menu.

"Joseline is out to fire anybody who's not showing up,

so you better get some shit clear with her before she crosses you out completely." Destiny nursed her Long Island.

"Fuck her! None speaking English ass bitch! She in there acting like she Dolla Bill from Player's Club and shit." Britney covered her moth when she realized she caused people to look in their direction.

"Her ass does be acting like him though. Talking about she wants her percentage. The bitch tried to take fifty percent from me the other night." Destiny nodded as she thought back on the night.

Joseline had been on one since the position got to her head. aA first Destiny didn't care, not until she thought she could take extra when it was Teddy's club and he had never done such things.

"She wishes! She doesn't run nothing cause we all know once Teddy comes home, she out the door like the other bitches he fucked with over the years. She isn't nobody special." Britney waved the waitress over to the table.

The waitress strolled over to the table with her notepad and pen already out to take orders. Service was fast and professional, which is why they chose the location.

"Hi, can I take your drink order?" the waitress asked with pen to paper.

"Yes, let me get a Mojito with an extra shot on the side. Matter of fact bring us all shots so we can turn up and out," Britney ordered.

"Okay, have you ladies decided on the food yet?" the waitress asked.

"Give us a minute to let Britney catch up with us on the drinks first, she just got here and we're not trying to rush our little time." Destiny capped off her drink and slid the glass aside.

"Bring me another drink too."

"Yeah, and me too, mine is kinda low," Skye said.

"Will do. I will be right up with your Mojito, shots and you two other drinks." The waitress scribbled something on the notepad and walked off.

"So, how are you? Where you been chick?" Destiny probed for more information, she wanted to know the real reason Britney stopped showing up for work. She refused to believe it was all due to Teddy not being there when money still had to be made.

"Chilling with my trick. He's been taking care of me very well, so I don't need to walk in that club right now. Shid, I guess you can say God blessed me." Britney laid her business on the table.

"Damn—that's what's up. I need to come up like that. Does he got any friends? And where did you meet him at?" Skye snapped her fingers and rolled her neck.

"I met him at a bar downtown during happy hour. All the white businessmen go there after work for drinks. We hit it off and been locked in since. You know I've been around all through the city, with all kinds of rich men. This one here is different." Britney bragged on her man like he was Jesus in the flesh.

"Damn! That's what's up. I need to be mingling," Skye said.

Destiny's mind was on Jackson, if what she heard about him was correct, he was going to take her away from the club and put her onto something bigger and better. She couldn't wait until she was able to brag about how she didn't have to work at the club if she didn't want to.

"I been trying to get y'all bitches to chill with me and get this real bag. Fuck that club. At least for now anyway, you know how niggas do. They fuck with you for a while then they get tired and find a new bitch to get their dick wet. So, the goal is to come up while I'm all there is on his mind," Britney said.

"You know I don't even be liking white men like that…" Skye balled her face.

"Shid, they got all the money and don't want hardly shit in return like these niggas. That's probably your problem now. You trying to stay down with the brothers when the brothers don't give a flying fuck about us like that." Britney humped her shoulders and looked over at Destiny.

"Yoooo! You just spoke some real shit. I'm ready," Skye said.

"Yeah, me too. Fuck this shit," Destiny chimed in.

"Cool. Check this out, I got a party for us, nothing but high-profiler business tricks going to be there. They only want pretty girls to hang out with." Britney popped her sunglass out her Prada bag and put them on.

"Well, you know it's us." Skye viewed Britney dumbfounded.

"Bet! It's tomorrow night though, so it's kind of short

notice. If you can't make it. I definitely understand," Britney said.

"I'm down and you already know that. Fuck a short notice. Show me to the money, ahhhhh!" Skye high fived Britney.

Destiny was too occupied by her phone to even chime into the conversation. Jackson had told her to hit him up if she was down for being in music videos. Shirell's words were still stuck in the back of her head like the last few conversations they had. Destiny typed a few words then cleared it out, she typed a few more words then backed out again.

"Destiny you down?" Skye bucked her eyes at Destiny.

"Huh? Oh, yeah, yeah, I'm going," Destiny said without removing her stare from the phone.

"Britney, do you know this white boy name, Jackson? He comes in the club sometimes." Destiny finally raised her eyes from the phone.

"Handsome, pretty eyes, killer smile? Always in the tailer-made suits?" Britney eyes lit up as she mentioned Jackson in the most poetic way.

"Yeah, that's him! He gave me his number," Destiny announced.

"Yeah, he used to always be in there. He wanted any dances from nobody, though, his boys did. Hell, he barely paid attention to any girl," Britney said.

The waitress came back around with the drinks; she sat Britney's drink on the table first then the shots, she then slid Destiny's drink to her, and Skye's drink followed.

"Enjoy!" the waitress said.

"Thanks," they said in unison.

"That's what I told her…" Skye took a sip of her drink.

"He talking about gettin' me some gigs in music videos cause he got a lot of celebrity friends. I still don't know what he does and if he's somebody I should be involved with," Destiny said.

"No one knows what he does, he hangs out with a lot of celebrities and they never charge him for drinks or VIP. He damn near walk in there like he's the boss even when Teddy was out," Britney informed Destiny of what she basically already knew about Jackson.

"I'm going to text him to see if he is for real." Destiny typed up another message to Jackson still unsure if she should press send or not.

"He does got money. I see the kind of cars he drives and he always fresh." Britney positioned the shots on the table in a line. "Let's take a shot, I think you could use one to get your nerves right, so you can go ahead and send that man a text."

"Definitely a shot!" Destiny said.

"Okayyyy! We have to stand for this shit here and I want to record….get over here." Britney held her phone in her left hand with the front camera facing them.

"Grab a shot!"

Destiny and Skye grabbed a shot. "One, two, three!"

Britney pressed record on the phone camera, and they downed the shots without a frown. "Yess, that's what I'm talking about, no weak bitches over here." They reoccupied their seat at the table without worrying about who were looking at them weird, they were there to spend money like everyone else.

"Text his ass and see what's up. Shit, I'm trying to do some videos too. You get on then you put me on. That's how the game go," Skye said.

"Yeah, I'm about to send it now." Destiny took a deep breath as she pulled the text message back up.

"I'm curious because he never talks to the dancers, so, I wonder is it really just videos he wants you for?" Britney giggled.

"I'm about to find out," Destiny pressed send on the text.

"How is Dj?" Britney changed the subject.

"Girl, he's good. Keeping Shirell on her toes since he's always with her, you know I'm barely home since I'm trying to rack up." Destiny left out the part where she was in some deep shit with his teacher and how Shirell wasn't pleased with being the only one who was responsible for his wellbeing while Destiny was all over the city.

"That's children for you, my son is bad as fuck. I'm happy my baby daddy don't mind giving me a break from time to time," Britney replied.

"At least you have a baby daddy, Dj's dad bailed before he was even born. And that very reason makes me not want to find my dad at all. Like maybe my momma is right, maybe my dad left me the same way Dj's dad left him," Destiny said.

"She's on drugs, right?" Britney asked.

"Yeah, has been for years," Destiny replied.

"So, why are you taking her word for anything. If you want to find your dad, then you need to find him." Britney pulled her glasses on top of her head.

"My new dude is a P.I., maybe he can help you, that's if you're serious about finding out about the other part of you."

"Oh, my God, that would be so great. I'm nervous though. he didn't want me then why would he now. And I hope the information she gave me is accurate." Destiny tried not to focus on it for too long and get her hopes up. She had bad experiences with men over the years, and since her dad never showed up for her, then he was the same good-for-nothing men that fit into the reason why she had trust issues when it came to the male species.

"You don't know that for sure. That's some bullshit your momma told you. From what you told me about her, she lies a lot. Besides, it's not about wanting you now or anything like that, you're grown. You're reaching out to know who he is, ya know?" Britney was one of the realest people Destiny encountered while being in Atlanta and they never really hung out.

"Yeah, you're right." Destiny agreed.

"Yeah, you need to talk to him for yourself and see if he wants to be in your life, period." Skye ended the conversation there. Her like Destiny never met her father, and although Destiny wanted to reach out to hers, Skye already got her closure with not having known that other part of her. He wasn't there when she was younger and now that she was grown, knowing him wasn't going to change anything or rewrite the past.

"I would love for my son to have at least one grand-parent or some type of father figure." Destiny slouched her shoulders.

"Cheer up! Where is the waitress? We need more drinks. We came here to relax not be sad bitch!" Skye tried to cheer Destiny up.

Once they got Destiny cheered up, they ordered their food and gossiped about the club some more and the party that Britney had line up for the next night. They stayed at the restaurant until the lunch rush was over then they departed to go on by their regular day. But the whole day all Destiny could do was hope and pray Jackson was really who he said he was and could get her on to something better than the strip club, so she would be able to tend to Dj the way a mother was supposed to.

CHAPTER Nine

"You've been home a lot lately…did you get fired?" Shirell sat the grocery sacks on the counter.

Destiny helped her put the groceries away without giving any insight on what was going on. For the past week, she wasn't sure what was happening in her life. She hadn't seen Jackson at the club while she worked her shift, and he hadn't responded to her text message. Skye told her not to sweat because Jackson seemed like a busy man and when the time was right, he was going to hit her up. There weren't too many women in Atlanta who were able to compete with Destiny, she had the model height and the video girl appearance. Plus, with the party she attended with Skye and Britney, she had a few men interested and ready to throw money at her.

"Is that a, yes?" Shirell furrowed her brow.

"Didn't you tell me that I needed to be here more with

Dj? I had to make a few sacrifices until I find another babysitter. I don't want you pulling all the slack and feeling like I'm using you and shit. I don't have time to be arguing anymore, Shirell." Destiny put the last item away.

"You let us stay here and that's more than enough.

"I never said you had to do that. All I asked was for you to be here more for Dj." Shirell took a seat at the table.

"I enjoy watching Dj, he may be the only anything close to a child that I receive in this world. I wanted to make sure you were spending time with him, because although I don't mind watching him, he does miss his mother from time to time."

"You know, Shirell, you love to go back on your words. You made me feel like crap the other week, throwing it up in my face about being responsible, now all sudden you love watching Dj and all that bullshit. Make up your mind. What's it's going to be?" Destiny's phone went off on the counter, and to her surprise, Jackson's name lit up the screen.

"Heyy, you!" Destiny answered.

"I received your message last week. I meant to hit you. Other business got in the way."

"I do have a video lined up for you." Jackson sounded drowned out by background music.

"Oh, for real? And when is that?" Destiny's heart dropped to the pit of her stomach.

She'd been pumping her head up since Jackson told her that he could get her own. Now that the ball was in her park and he had some things lined up for her, she wasn't sure she had what it took to be in some video for the world to see. It was easy at the club, all she had to do was entertain the crowd and be on her way once her set was done. Nobody told her how to dance or what to dance to.

"Tomorrow. I have a friend from Atlanta that's coming out here to shoot a video and he's letting me put it all together," Jackson replied.

Destiny viewed Shirell with a huge smile. She had been in a slump all week and all she needed was for Jackson to hit her up to change the whole vibe.

"Tomorrow?" Destiny questioned.

Her and Shirell was in the middle of a conversation about Dj before Jackson called. Destiny made it established that she was making sacrifices for Dj, so that meant Shirell was off the hook from watching him. She wanted to take the last ten minutes back; an opportunity landed in her hand, one that could change her and Dj's life if she played her cards right.

"Is that a problem?" Jackson asked.

"No, I'm available. You have my word," Destiny assured.

"Okay, that's straight. I'm going to send you the details over and the contract." Jackson ended the call.

"Ohhhh my fucking god!" Destiny screamed with the phone pressed to her chest.

Shirell witnessed how Destiny got excited over the smallest things, so she waited before she gave any kind of reaction or ask about what she had going on. Part of her didn't want to know the news at all, due to her always having to sacrifice on Destiny's behalf when she received bigger opportunities. While she was trying to help Destiny get on her feet, her desires crumbled. She put her life on hold to help raise Dj as if she played a part in creating him.

"Remember the guy I told you about—The one who works with all kinds of celebrities and stuff?" Destiny jumped slightly. "That was him. He told me that he has a video for me tomorrow!"

"That sounds promising." Shirell removed herself from the table.

When Destiny decided to work at the strip club, she said it was only going to be for a short time. She started out working only the weekends to her being gone every day. She had the money to show for it, Shirell, however, couldn't overlook nonexistent presence in Dj's life.

"Now there you go—what's the deal now?" Destiny paced around the kitchen as she sent a text to Skye informing her about the good news.

"I think you should search for a normal job with a decent schedule. I know people that know people who will work with you. Destiny, nothing ever ends well in the entertainment industry. You know that. Look at where all the young women end up…either on drugs or back out on the streets. Some even end up in those abusive relationships pimped out to rich men." Shirell grew tired of trying to beat sense into Destiny's head. Destiny was grown with her own mind, and sometimes Shirell felt like she was overstepping whenever she tried to dictate her life.

"Can you stop with this bullshit! Be happy for me this

one time. I know all my recent decisions weren't the best. I think this one is going to play out differently. I get in the game, work my way up and find something to invest in." Destiny had it all mapped out, how she would come in as a video vixen and get out.

"I am happy for you, Destiny. I've always been happy for you." Shirell took a deep breath.

"I care about you. I truly care about you and your well-being. You moved out here with me. I feel responsible for your well-being. If something happens to you or Dj, everyone back home will have mean things to say about me." Shriell tried hard to piece together her thoughts. Destiny was heading down a dark road, even an average person could see it coming.

"I don't want you somewhere dead and Dj being sent to live with a man he never met or someone who doesn't give a damn about him."

"Oh, I hear you, Shirell." Destiny brushed the words off.

"But can you watch him for me tomorrow, or do I need to find a babysitter?"

"You got it." Shirell shut down from the argument. The more Destiny made poor choices, the easier it was for Shirell to see Tammy in her. The curse of the mother had become the child.

"I owe you big time, and this is about to change my life for the better. Wait and see." Destiny darted out of the kitchen upstairs to hit up Skye. They had a lot of shopping to do before the video shoot. She wanted to look and feel her best, and there was nothing fresh outfits couldn't fix.

Skye hit her back up and agreed to link up at Lenox Square. Out of all the places, there were to be in Atlanta, Lenox was the place to be for locals and tourists. Everybody that was somebody made it their business to shop there.

Before Destiny headed that way, she picked up Dj and drove him back to the house to be with Shirell until she made it back. The deal was for Shirell to watch him while she was at the video shoot. However, Destiny somehow persuaded her into taking on the job once more.

"Bitchhh!" Skye screamed across the mall as Destiny approached her.

If nobody ever stood in Destiny's corner to make her feel like the sexiest woman walking, it was her hands down. Whenever Skye found a friend, she connected with, she made sure they felt that connection to their core. Because at the end of the day, she knew that if the connection was genuine, they would do the same for her too.

"Nooo, bitch, look at you. Who the fuck done dropped commas on you?" Destiny grabbed Skye into a tight embrace as if they hadn't seen each other in months.

"No, bump all of that. You haven't even shot the video or fucked that nigga, and you're glowing." Skye pulled away from Destiny with a smile.

"I don't know, I feel so good, though. Like life is finally going in the right direction." Destiny looped her arm into Skye's, and they walked along the mall like two high school girls on a mission to find the hottest attire for the hottest party of the year.

"You know you have to put me on once you have your feet in the door. Don't be making that new money and forget about me." Skye jogged Destiny's memory.

"How could I forget about the one bitch who looked out for me the first day at the club? You know I got you, boo. Don't be doing all that extra shit. You put me on to money outside of the club, so it's only right for me to do the same when the time presents itself," Destiny said.

"Okayyy, that's what I like to hear. I know my bitch got my back." They passed by a few storefronts that were crowded, the lines reached from the front of the stores down to the front entrances.

Skye nudged Destiny as a lightbulb seemed to go off in her mind. "I forgot to tell you that Teddy's baby momma showed up at the club. She almost dragged Joseline. Teddy normally breaks her off money for his children, but while he's away, Joseline oversees taking care of all of that. She wasn't giving his baby momma anything for the children."

"Did she up the money?" Destiny asked as she visualized the scene. Joseline had been rubbing everyone wrong and trying to run things her way and not the way Teddy wanted things to go.

"It was either up the money or get fucked up, and you know Joseline isn't about that life. She upped the money quicker than that man from Friday upped that bike to Debo." Skye broke down in laughter.

"I wish I was there to see that shit. I keep saying that

Joseline is going to get that ass handed to her if she doesn't change her attitude and the way she treats people. She knows damn well she was supposed to give that woman some money for the children. She acts like she's Teddy's wife or something." Destiny couldn't wait until the club days were long behind her and she didn't have to deal with women like Joseline. The sooner she got away from the club the quicker life would pan out.

"Yeah, you should've been there. It was a whole mess in that club. Joseline was hollering for security. Tey didn't move not one bit because they know if they touched her Teddy would have their head when he got out. He doesn't play about his baby momma." Skye viewed a window display wide eyed.

"If you ask me, Teddy's baby momma is the real HBIC."

"Damn!" Destiny managed to summon as she scrolled Dominque's Instagram for the first time since leaving Memphis. She was curious to know how things turned out after she left. Before she had the breakdown, Dominique was kicking it with D. Wallace, going behind her back, trying to come up.

"Why is your face tight like that?" Skye asked.

"Girl, nothing."

Destiny felt ill as she lurked on Dominique's page. The further she scrolled, the more she regretted not dragging her through the mud. Dominique was living the good life; she still had the title of being D. Wallace's girl. From the looks of it, he'd moved back to Memphis, and they shared two children around the same age as Dj.

Destiny's body boiled as she tried her best to pull her attention away from the phone. It was bad enough D. Wallace wanted nothing to do with Dj when he was born. Then there he was playing daddy to Dominque's children, who weren't too far off in years.

"There's definitely something. You look like you're going to throw up." Skye read the vibe.

"Remember I told you that my best friend was sneaking with the man that got me knocked up? Turns out they're married with two children. When I got knocked up, he wasn't ready to be a dad and all that bullshit." Destiny hadn't thought about the situation between Dominque and D. Wallace in years. Now that it was fresh on her mind, the pain felt like it did the first day she found out about the betrayal.

"Fuck them trifling ass people." Skye directed Destiny into one of the high-end stores.

Skye had dealt with all kinds of betrayal, she had to learn that nobody owed her anything in life but herself. That kept her going and not being behind bars for placing a bullet in somebody's head.

"Yeah, you're right."

Destiny redirected her attention to what lied ahead, she was doing something that Dominque would never do. As she thought about it, she realized it had been like that since the start. Dominque had no real talent, her only talent involved laying on her back trying to get money from a man.

As they shopped for new attire for Destiny's video shoot, Jackson sent over the business documents she had to sign before showing up on set. He told her that she could get a lawyer to look over the fine print but clarified that it would be a waste of money since there wasn't any fine print involved.

Sean, the director, sat behind a monitor with a few other people as the rapper, Young Flyo lip-sync as Destiny danced on him. She was all over him like they were the perfect two. As the lights shined on her, Young Flyo stared down at her with lust in his eyes, made her feel like she was on top of the world. Jackson hyped her up and flirted around like a schoolboy via text whenever she went on break and sent him a picture. Attention wasn't new, receiving it without being on stage felt better.

"Cut! That's a wrap, guys," Sean shouted across the studio.

Destiny walked away from the greenscreen as Jackson made his presence known without murmuring a word. He was the only white man on the scene dressed as he worked at a corporate office. And the way he presented himself, one would assume that he took pride in how he appeared to others.

"What's up, man? How is everything going today?" Jackson shook Sean's hand.

"It went well. Your girl did great too. She's hot as fuck. Gave me something to look at while I did my job." Sean chuckled.

"Perfect." Jackson's thumbs slid over the screen quickly.

"I'm thinking about using her for a few more coming up. I can't wait to shoot her again. I was even thinking about shooting her alone for one. Not no music video, more like a teaser." Sean packed up his equipment.

"Cool, she will be ready." Jackson was still glued to his phone.

Sean passed Jackson a white envelope. "Here's the money for the product."

"It's all here?" Jackson tucked the phone away and pulled out another.

"Now, you know it is. Don't do me like that, man. I never short-changed you. I know better." Sean shook his head in disbelief.

"I don't put shit past nobody, you know that. A friend today may try to put a bullet in my head tomorrow." Jackson placed the envelope into the inside of his suit pocket.

"And I want you to mak—" Jackson cut off as he acknowledged Destiny's presence.

"Hey, you," Destiny greeted.

"What's up? I heard you did a good job for your first video." Jackson smirked.

"Yeah, you know I was born with it." Destiny poked Jackson in the arm.

"Fo sho, she is a natural," Sean complimented. He winked at Destiny.

"Destiny, I will touch basis with you soon. Good job! New artists hitting the city soon and that'll need your service."

"Thank you, Sean," Destiny replied.

When she first walked in the building, she was chatting away with everybody as she hung around them all the time. It was the same thing she did when she first started at Teddy's club. Skye snatched her up quickly, and made it clear that everybody in the club wasn't to be trusted and not everybody needed to know her life story. Her job there was to dance and sell a fantasy to men who couldn't get any real action in the real world. Making friends at the club was a quick way to get her throat slit.

"No problem." Sean finished packing his equipment.

"How you feel?" Jackson asked. Destiny had his full attention the way she did when she first officially met him.

"I feel alright." Destiny tried not to do too much around Jackson or make him feel bigger than he needed to for putting her on. Destiny witnessed firsthand where that got her with D. Wallace; she placed him on a pedestal.

"You thought I was playing. Your first video with a major artist and director. You're already winning out here. You'll be out of that club before the end of next week," Jackson said.

Destiny hadn't given the club any thought all day, her

next shift was for the following night. Joseline had done well by her by allowing her to take off a few days to handle things at the house with Shirell. Which didn't help a damn thing, the time away from work caused more problems than a few.

"Yeah, yeah, that's what's up. Sooo, you got my money for this or what?" Destiny said.

Jackson talked a lot; nothing was all good without Destiny seeing her money. Teddy peeped when she first started at the club that she wasn't like any of the other girls who worked for him. He had to do way more than break her off a little money, she wanted all her money or she was going to walk.

Jackson chuckled. "Chill, baby girl, I got you. I see you about your bread, shit, me too."

Jackson never been in two feet of a woman like Destiny, most women trusted him off the fly. All he had to do was shoot them big dreams, and show them how he ran things in the city, they threw themselves in his direction.

Jackson reached into his suit pocket and revealed a band of money thicker than Destiny had ever laid eyes on in the club. "You must be used to guys being dishonest with you?"

"Words mean nothing to me," Destiny replied.

Jackson pulled some money out of the band and handed it over to Destiny, he was aware how much women brought in at Teddy's club, even the top dancers, and it wasn't nearly as much he paid her for the video.

"Damn!" Destiny said.

Jackson pulled her to him; he looked down at her as if he wanted to fuck her right there inside of the studio amongst everybody. "So, what kind of other time can I pay for?"

"What can you afford?" Destiny whispered.

"I can afford a lot…I need some alone time with you," Jackson said.

"We might can do that." Destiny felt her entire body throb. She hadn't wanted a man as bad as she wanted Jackson in years.

"Let's do it now. Come on, let's get out of here," Jackson suggested.

When Destiny walked into the hotel room, she didn't get all excited the way she did when D. Wallace took her to the Four Seasons years ago. She saw a lot of fancy hotels by then and hung out with a few rich people. So, what Jackson showed her wasn't something that made her panties wet anymore.

"Is it red?" Destiny asked.

Up until that day, she hadn't gone to any hotel with a white man or even watched white porn. She did hear some of the girls in the club talking about their experiences. Most of them never mentioned what the color looked like, they did mention the size, and from what she heard, it was all lies that white men weren't packing too.

"Red? Who the hell ever told you that shit?" Jackson undressed and revealed himself.

Destiny looked down in amazement, it was a bright pink color with a length that suppressed D. Wallace's and the other men she fooled around with over the years. Judging Jackson from appearance, she never would've assumed he packed a weapon.

"Oh, you coming like that?" Destiny's eyes bucked.

"Yeah, don't be believing all that shit they say about us. Not all are lacking in that department. As you can see, I'm not." Jackson said

"I see," Destiny said.

"Bring it to me."

Jackson chuckled. "Nah you come over here to me."

"Say less Mr. Long Pipe Master." Destiny made her way over to Jackson.

She was ready to feel him inside of her. Since she'd been working at the club, she hadn't been getting any bedroom action. She was too focused on making more to even ponder on the feeling of being under a man. Sex brought problems she refused to deal with. It sure as hell costed her dreams years ago.

Jackson picked Destiny up and carried her into the bathroom. Destiny saw it done in the movies. The man would pick up the woman and then make love to her. She hadn't experienced it in real life, not until Jackson. The men she did lay down with ripped her clothes off and skipped fourplay. Within ten minutes, they found their climax and left her high and dry. Every time she finished messing around, she had to please herself afterward, sometimes with the man still in the room. She never cared to spare their ego then they refused to give a damn about her getting off.

"Oh, you doing it like that?" Destiny said.

Jackson directed Destiny to wrap her legs around his waist as he turned on the double-head shower. The water steamed up the bathroom, and all Destiny could see was Jackson's outline.

He lowered her onto her feet in the shower and then pinned her against the wall. He sucked on her neck while cupping her breast. He dipped low to suck each nipple with aggression. Destiny's pussy juiced as Jackson took his time with her, and all the problems she faced subsided. She wanted him to explore every part of her being, discover things about her body that she hadn't.

"Ouuu, let me feel you in me," Destiny whispered.

"You will." Jackson placed Destiny upon his shoulders and ate her pussy like the main course at a five-star restaurant. His tongue explored every part of her pussy, traveling places no man had.

"Ummm, shit. You going to make me cum." Destiny held onto Jackson's head. Her chest lifted, and she collapsed into an orgasm that almost made her float to heaven.

Jackson lowered Destiny. He lathered her body as she did the same for him. While he was focused on her getting her clean, she was busy trying to get him back excited. She knew what his tongue action was about now she wanted to know did he know what he was doing in the other department.

"You can't get back hard?" Destiny had any doubt in her mind that she was the baddest woman he ever messed around with, so him not getting hard threw her for a curve.

"Nah, I can. I know how to control myself. I have what most men don't, and that's control. When you can control your impulses, you can do anything." Jackson turned off the shower. He led Destiny out into the room. He guided her onto the bed as he directed her to get on top.

Destiny positioned Jackson's dick inside. "Ummm, it's huge."

Destiny slid further down his dick and all she could do was moan. He filled her up to compacity. She bounced up and down as he held onto her waist and met her rhythm.

"Ahhh damn! You take it good, baby girl. Turn that ass around and let me see it." Jackson grabbed Destiny by the throat, he squeezed her enough to be the one in charge of if she lived or not then he released and helped her turn into the reverse cowgirl potion. As she went to bouncing, he smacked her ass turned red.

"Oh, fuck, oh fuck!" Destiny moaned. Jack gripped her waist tight as he could as he released inside of her. In that moment she was thankful that she was now on birth control and didn't have to worry about another Dj popping up and having to do it on her own.

"Damn." Jackson said breathlessly.

Destiny glanced over at the clock on the nightstand, it was past nine o'clock, and Shirell had texted her earlier in the day about her plans for the evening and to be back at a certain time. Destiny hopped up out the bed. She was supposed to go shoot a video and be back home, but she was in the hotel room with Jackson while Shirell played the mother role with Dj again.

"Fuck. I have to go." Destiny threw her clothes on quicker than they had come off.

"Alright, I wish you could stay, I wouldn't mind getting more of that in the morning." Jackson viewed Destiny as he lay on the bed butt naked.

"That's some good pussy."

"Yeah, I've been told," Destiny said.

"Is there anything you not good at?" Jackson asked.

"Not really. I have many talents," Destiny replied.

"I would like to know all about them," Jackson said.

Destiny puckered her lips. "I'm sure you would."

"I'm serious." Jackson hopped out of the bed and pulled Destiny to him.

"I want to know everything about you. Where you from. Your likes. Your dislikes…everything." Jackson never been the type of man to hold his feelings inside whenever he dug a woman's style. He was secure in himself as a man, he learned long ago that a man who was true to himself was to be trusted.

"Sure. I heard this before. I'm not trying to go down that road again. I'm focused on me, and my son. I'm securing a bag for our future." Destiny pulled away from Jackson.

"Why don't you roll with me?" Jackson asked.

"Roll with you and do what—more music videos?" Destiny rolled her neck.

"Sometimes. But nah…get money with me. Leave the club, you don't need it." Jackson pulled Destiny to him again.

"Leave the club? I have a son I have to take care and so far, all you did was get me in one music video and the other ones not even set in stone." Destiny shook her head at the way Jackson tried to take her fast.

"Trust, being with me, you will make way more money than that club. Besides, Teddy owes me so much money. I practically own that damn club. If I want to shut it down, all I have to do is snap my fingers, it's over. You don't want to be caught up there when it's heading for closure."

Jackson laid it all out in simple terms for Destiny to understand. Teddy was in hot water with Jackson and a lot of other people. If the club closed, that meant she was out of a job. There were clubs lined up ready to offer her position, but she wasn't familiar with anyone there.

Jackson strolled over to the minibar and poured him a glass of whiskey.

"Like that? You can shut the club down." Destiny placed her hands on her hips. It sounded like a threat to her if she didn't agree to his offer. She couldn't wrap her mind around what kind of man would shut down an entire club to get her with him.

"You still haven't told me what the hell you do? You probably rob people or some bullshit."

Jackson gave a sly smirk. "I will tell you when you let

me know that you're ready to go to the next level." Jackson took a swig from the glass.

"I will think about it. I have to go; my son is with the sitter." Destiny swung her purse over her shoulder.

"Don't think too long," Jackson said.

"I hope you got your American Express ready cause I'm not cheap to roll with." Destiny headed to the door.

"I have something better…cash and lots of it." Jackson took another swig from the whiskey glass.

"Remember, scared money don't make no money."

Destiny glanced back at him and flashed a smile before she exited the room. She left Jackson with a lot on his mind while he gave her a huge decision.

CHAPTER Ten

Shirell sat at the table helping Dj with his homework when Destiny walked in the door with shopping bags that looked like she had robbed a few stores. Shirell viewed the bags with her nose turned in the air in disgust. She never been the one to question Destiny's spending habits or why she bought more than she needed. However, she did try to talk about the importance of being responsible with finances.

"Don't start Shirell." Destiny placed the shopping bags on the counter.

Dj hadn't even looked up at Destiny, the more days she was away from him, the more he grew accustomed to it and clung to Shirell.

"Business ran longer than I thought it would." Destiny rubbed Dj's head and leaned down to kiss him on the forehead.

"How you doing champ?"

"Fine," Dj murmured.

"Somebody needs to start with you." Shirell followed Destiny out of the kitchen and up the stairs.

Shirell missed her date due to Destiny not staying true to her word. She asked Shirell to look after Dj for a little while. Shirell made it clear that she had plans and to be on time, Destiny did horrible with time management. Shirell hoped that the guy understood why she couldn't make their date.

"Why are you following me?" Destiny complained.

Shirell allowed Destiny to enter the room first; she closed the door behind them. "I'm tired of this, I'm not his mother. You are."

"I know I'm his damn mother. It's me, not you. I know that Shirell. So, what's this all about now?" Destiny plumped onto the bed.

"Yeah, you have been a great mother. I bet you would win mother of the year," Shirell said sarcastically as she fueled around the room trying to find the right words to light a fire underneath Destiny to make her get her life together. She was hopping from one dead end to the next, hoping for a quick come-up.

"I don't care what you think. I'm so tired of you. You are supposed to be one of my best friends and have my back." Destiny couldn't believe the words that oozed from Shirell's lips. She had been cutting deep with her words lately. Destiny was ready to write her off as a friend, they were living two different lives that neither understood.

"You can't see how much I have your damn back? I let y'all move in and stay with me. I keep Dj and help him with his homework while you are out with God knows who. Yeah, I have your back. I didn't plan on taking your place as a mother." Shirell pinched the bride of her nose as she heaved a heavy sigh.

"No one asked you to take my place as his mother," Destiny said.

Shirell placed her hands on her hips as she viewed Destiny. Had she been any other person, they would've turned her reported her to CPS and had Dj taken away for child negligence or try to get him in their custody as guardian. Shirell knew Destiny couldn't be a proper mother from the jump since she never had a good example herself.

"But I am! You don't do shit, you don't help him with his homework. He barely sees you; on top of that, his teacher has put another note for a parent-teacher conference in his bag which you missed the first one she put in there. I assumed you showed up one day and told her some bullshit and left." Shirell watched Destiny rise from the bed and walk out of the door.

"This is fucking childish."

"I don't have time for this shit," Destiny complained.

"You are unbelievable, Destiny," Shirell yelled.

Destiny turned to face Shirell on the stairs. "I'm tired of you looking down on me. You don't know what the hell I've been through. You haven't lived my life or have to be a single mother."

"It's the same story from you. You blame everything on your childhood and your cracked-out momma. You're not the only one who has been through some shit. My mom wasn't the best, but you don't see me blaming her for everything or my daddy." Shirell viewed the woman whom she once thought she understood. All Destiny did was enable her bullshit by playing the role of a victim.

"How long are you going to be a victim?"

"Sorry, I can't be as perfect and strong as you. My life is a little more complicated. I have a child that I care for. I got to do what I have to do." Destiny defended herself.

"No, you have a child that you don't keep. I been watching him since you moved out here. If you spent half the time with Dj as you do those tricks and hoes you hang out with, I wouldn't have anything to say. I'm tired being your crutch." Shirell allowed every emotion she'd been feeling towards the situation to spill. She grew tired of allowing Destiny to use her as a steppingstone. To her, they weren't anything close to friends anymore; they were only roommates because they barely passed any words to each other.

"My crutch? How the hell you been my crutch?" Destiny frowned.

"Yeah, your crutch! You've been chasing basketball players since I met you that semester, and you finally got one, and look where you ended up, in the strip club and a single mother. Good job, Destiny," Shirell argued.

Shirell knew that nothing good would come out of Destiny following behind Dominique like a puppy and not taking college seriously. Instead of studying, she was tagging along to some party Dominique got them invites to. If it wasn't a party, then it was at some other place that had men all around. Shirell turned down their offers to hang out numerous times. Looking at Destiny and what happened in her life, she couldn't be more thankful for standing firm on her decision.

"Wow! You try so hard to act innocent. In college, you were looking for the highest bidder, sugar daddy. Now you walk around with your glasses and a nice job and got the nerve to look down on me—" Destiny stopped herself before she said something that would cause Shirell to slip into depression.

"You know what, yeah, I had them to get through school but that was for a time. You're still doing the same shit," Shirell fussed.

"You don't have to be my crutch anymore because I'm moving out." Destiny started back down the stairs. She'd put up more than she could bear with Shirell. If all she was going to come home to is complaining, then she had to change her environment. Atlanta was big and finding a nanny wasn't as hard as it seemed. There were a lot of people looking for decent pay. If Jackson was a man of his word, paying someone a nice salary to look after Dj while she handled business would be easy.

"Where are you going?" Shirell asked.

"Don't worry, we will be out by the end of the week. We don't fucking need you anymore for shit. I won't have to deal with you throwing bullshit up in my face every chance you get." Destiny stomped into the kitchen. She put all Dj's books into his backpack and ordered him to put on his shoes.

"Where the hell are you taking him? He must finish his homework. He has school in the morning, he hasn't even had a bath yet," Shirell complained.

"Don't worry. We will be back for our things," Destiny said.

Destiny grabbed Dj by the arm and forced him out of the house. He tried to break away from her grip and run back inside to Shirell, however, his strength was no match for Destiny. Shirell ran in front of Destiny, and tried to grab Dj.

"You are a selfish person to drag him out of this house. I hope God have mercy on you, Destiny." Shirell wiped at her tears, although life had become hard for her trying to juggle work and deal with Dj, she hadn't thought up what she would do without him being there. She hadn't asked for Destiny to move out, all she wanted was extra help around the house with Dj and for Destiny to be involved.

"Forget your God! He hasn't done shit for me, so I don't need him," Destiny said.

"I hope you never need him then." Shirell placed her hand on her chest. It was hard enough having to witness Dj being in a slump some nights when Destiny promised to spend time with him after work but never showed.

Shirell threw her hands up in defeat and headed inside. That night, she had to leave it in God's hand and pray that Dj didn't end up hurt or in the system.

“Mommy where are we going? I want to stay with, Shirel—” Dj cut off when Destiny slung the car door open and forced him inside.

“Mommy got this,” Destiny said, not sure if she believed her own words.

Although Destiny had money stashed back, it didn’t eliminate the fact that finding a place to stay on short notice was a challenge within itself. She thought about calling Skye then decided against it since Skye had her own life. Skye took care of herself and lived in a one-bedroom apartment, there was no way three people would be able to stay there.

“I got this,” Destiny said as she sat behind the steering wheel.

Deciding to move out of Shirell’s house wasn’t a thought-out plan, but there was no going back because she wanted to make a point, to show Shirell that she wasn’t a crutch.

Destiny managed to find a babysitter thanks to Britney putting her on to some woman who lived out in Decatur who didn’t mind taking in more children. She ran a daycare right out of the house and had been doing it for two decades.

Dj had a fit when he realized that he would be staying with a woman he knew nothing about, he had a meltdown as he begged her to take him to Shirell. Destiny shook him off and left him there to cry alone in a strange environment, if the word got back to Shirell, hell was going to boil over for Destiny.

"Why you so quiet over there?" Jackson woke Destiny from her deep thoughts that was riddled in guilt. Long as Dj been alive, she hadn't ever left him with any strangers and for the years she been out in Atlanta, Shirell made sure he never had to be left with someone he didn't know.

"Oh, my bad. It's just things are gettin' out of hand for me." Destiny leaned the seat back. She looked over at Jackson with a smirk.

"What do you need me to do?"

"It's easy, I need you to go in these clubs and get my packages from the owners. I will give you the name to ask for in each club. You get the package, you hand the package over to me," Jackson said.

Jackson hit Destiny up the day after the video shoot, he told her that he had other business that she could be involved with if she was willing to get her hands dirty. Since she was out on her own without any help from Shirell, she agreed without thinking things through. She had to make money to get Dj a better babysitter, someone who could come over to the apartment and sit with him while she was out working. She still had to find them an apartment to live in.

"You still haven't told me what you do or what I'm gettin' myself into." Destiny thought up a thousand things Jackson could've had under his sleeves.

Jackson sighed. "I got business dealings with a lot of the clubs around here. I let some businesses borrow money and in exchange they let me sell my party drugs and clean my money." Jackson glanced over at Destiny.

"Anything else you want to know?"

"You are a loan shark and a drug dealer?" Destiny's bottom lip almost hit the seat.

"I am whatever that makes me money. See Destiny, that's the difference between someone like me and someone like you. I know exactly who I am and what it takes to get what I want." Jackson picked up his phone and sent a quick text before he refocused on the conversation.

"I know who I am." Destiny rolled her eyes hard as she could.

Jackson knew so little about her, but he sat there and assumed that she didn't know herself. Over the years, that's what the search was about, to find Destiny.

"Then who are you, baby girl?" Jackson asked.

Destiny sat in deep thought, she'd been searching yet she never found who she really was. She was aware of her likes and dislikes, but she didn't know herself to the core.

"Right. Look, I got some of the girls in the club pushing that need extra money. I provide a lot of big names some of my party products," Jackson said.

"You know everyone, so, is that how you got me in the music video? You're not a manager obviously." Destiny pressed her head against the headrest, Shirell told her to be careful and to not trust Jackson until she asked around about him, now she was riding shotgun as he explained to her what he did for a living. None of it sounded like the type of shit she needed to be involved with.

"Bingo. You are catching on fast. Lots of people owe me, only thing it takes is for me to demand them my wants and they scatter like roaches to fulfill it." Jackson chuckled.

"That's why you always in Teddy's club running up your tab and why Joseline let you have your way." Destiny stomach turned.

Back home in Memphis she steered clear of the dope boys, nothing good every came out of it. Whenever the dope boys had beef, their girls or family paid the price of a bullet to the head. Destiny always said that it would be a cold day in hell before she agreed to be the first lady of the trap; that day arrived quicker than she thought.

"Look, I provide a lot of things in the club atmosphere. Teddy owes me so much money I own that club. I get to do whatever I want and that includes cleaning my money. For now, I need you to do what I need you to do. You can make some money to take care of you and your kid, everything is kosher." Jackson fired up a Cuban cigar and leaned the seat back. He took a drag and blew out smoke halos.

"I'm down, but I need to get my place quick. And find a better babysitter for my son, I can't have him down in the hood like that," Destiny said.

"What's going on with your crib?" Jackson asked.

"When I first moved here, I moved in with a friend. Shit isn't working out right now. I need to bounce by the end of the week. I'm living inside of a hotel right now with my son and I don't like that," Destiny informed Jackson.

"Say less, baby girl. We will have you a new crib tomorrow. Search for a sitter and I'll pay her daily to watch your son and help him with school, if need be," Jackson made it all sound simple; Destiny allowed her worries to subside.

"Ouuuu, like that?" Destiny exclaimed.

"Where we going right now?"

"Your first pickup. Sit back and take this ride with me. I'm going to introduce you to the entire game. I feel like I can trust you for some reason. We going to be like Bonnie and Clyde." It sounded like Jackson was trying to run game, Destiny took it for what it was and decided to see it through.

"Yeah, the Oreo version," Destiny laughed.

"That'll work too," Jackson said.

Being with Jackson made time move quick, Destiny's head was in the clouds with him, and he'd done everything he said he would. Although, she was out pushing loads for him in the clubs and other business establishments. He still had videos lined up for her, and the house he promised she would receive fell right into her lap with a live-in nanny. Her need for Shirell diminished. While she was out working to make money to support her and Dj, her phone didn't go off demanding she come home like a mother.

Destiny stayed out six days a week all night every night,

from club to club and video shoot to the next, she was back and forth from Atlanta to California at least three times per month. Shirell called to speak with Dj a few times, but she never got Destiny on the phone. Destiny watched Shirell's call and sent each one straight to voicemail. She wiped her hands clean of the friendship.

"Here we go." Destiny hopped out of the black Jaguar that she purchased a month after getting her money right.

She crossed the street to the club that Jackson had business with. It was a nice size club owned by an ex-cartel member. All week, she asked Jackson to tag along with her on the pickup, she thought it best that he be present when she set some things straight, because the man owed Jackson too much money not to make a payment.

Jackson made it seem like he ran the entire show. She witnessed how men trembled in his presence and all the projects he managed to put together for her within a few months. She also saw how some people played in his face and gave him sob stories as to why they couldn't catch up on their payments.

"Where's Manuel?" Destiny asked the man that stood in front of the club on guard.

Jackson informed her how tight security was at Manuel's club, he had been in with some dangerous people, he trusted nobody since everybody was an opp in his eyes.

The guard viewed Destiny up and down, he flashed his grills at her like she was some woman that came there looking for a man. "What the fuck you want Manuel for?"

"This is a personal visit, unless you want your guts splattered over this fucking club, you best point me in his direction." Destiny pulled out a Glock with a suppressor. She pressed it against the man's stomach between the over-sized jacket she wore.

"Calm your nerves shawty," the man's voice trembled.

"Where is he?" Destiny asked.

"He's in the back. I'll take you to him," the man said.

"Alright, let's go."

Destiny kept the gun aimed but not enough to make it noticeable. Jackson told her to go in there professional, but since Manuel hadn't paid Jackson back in months, she took it upon herself to make him sweat the money up. Jackson knew that people who were in debt with him, belonged to him until Jesus' second coming.

"He's in there." the man pointed Destiny to a door at the end of the hallway past the restrooms.

"Thank you for being so kind," Destiny replied and let the man walk away in peace.

She opened the door casually and walked in. Manuel sat in front of a big screen downing a beer like he was on top of the world. Jackson had been trying to get a hold of him for months and all it took was for him to break through security to find him.

"Nice tv you have here. How much did it cost you?" Destiny took a seat on the opposite side of Manuel.

Since Jackson let her in, she'd been a one-woman army, most of the men liked her while others tucked their tails and told Jackson not to ever send her their way again.

"Who da fawk are you?" Manuel said in a thick Spanish accent.

"I can be your friend or your worst nightmare." Destiny placed the cold Glock to his temple.

"What's this about?" Manuel asked.

"You owe Jackson some money and I come to collect. He's been letting you off the hook but I'm not having it. You not paying is taking money out of his pocket, which in return takes money from me. I want you to up at least half of what you owe him then by the end of the week I'll come collect the other half." Destiny smiled as the adrenaline overtook her soul.

"I thought Jackson understood what I have going on here. We've been doing business for years; I never had this problem with him. Money has been slow coming in the club. Customers aren't throwing money at the dancers the way they used to. I don't know if you saw, but nobody is in here at the bar telling the bartender their sob stories," Manuel complained.

"I don't give a fuck about business being slow. Business been slow around the whole fucking city and they still paying up. I'm not leaving here unless I get the money or if you refuse to, I'll place a hot one right in your head. I mean, either way Jackson will win." Destiny pressed the gun harder against Manuel's head.

"Okay, I'll get you the money. You tell Jackson that after I pay him off, I'm not doing business with him anymore." Manuel looked across the room at his gun that rested underneath the tv. If he somehow got hands on the gun, he was going to send Destiny back to Jackson in a body bag for running up in his club demanding shit when they were supposed to have had an understanding.

"Don't even think about pulling any bullshit on me either. I'm quick on the trigger, don't let this pretty face fool you. You think I came in here not knowing how you roll. You an ex-cartel member, you still have some people backing you, you run a lot of shit across the border, I know you. The real you, but I don't give a fuck, because right now, I have one up on you." Destiny surprised herself how she handled Manuel.

"I thought the game made you street smart, never be caught slipping or you'll meet your end."

"Okay, I have to give you props. You have heart. I wonder where the fawk, Jackson found you?" Manuel chuckled.

"Are you going to let me go get the money for you?"

Manuel put his hands in the air to show Destiny he wasn't in the mood to meet her on the level she walked in on. He wanted to get back to his movie and revamp the way he was going to bring hell down on Jackson and her for crossing him. He ran a business; Jackson knew him well enough to know that the money would eventually come up somehow.

"Of course…walk." Destiny kept the Glock aimed at Manuel's head.

She followed him as he walked across the office over to a safe that sat five feet off the floor. Most clubs Destiny visited had the safes placed in the wall. Destiny watched

Manuel input a few numbers on the safe, the knob turned, and he twisted it open. Money was neatly stacked to the top, amounting more than what he owed Jackson. Destiny widened her eyes as she viewed the money. Since being with Jackson her hand touched all kinds of money, she never laid eyes on that much.

"Damn. You have the money all here, and you choose to not to pay Jackson?" Destiny shook her head.

"It's not that simple. This money keeps things afloat; I have many other business affairs and people I owe." Manuel placed bands of money in a brown duffel bag. Paying Jackson partial of the money owed was sure to put him in hot water with other business partners who didn't mind catching a plane from Mexico to Atlanta.

"Looks like you need to be a bit smarter," Destiny suggested.

"You may be right," Manuel said in defeat.

"It's all there?" Destiny asked.

"It should be. If it's not, you know where to find me." Manuel gave a sly smirk.

Manuel tossed the duffel bag across the room to Destiny. She slung it over her shoulder and headed out the door.

"Be good." Destiny walked out of the office on a mission to make it to the other side of the city. Jackson hit her up earlier in the day and told her after she paid Manuel a visit to meet up with him.

CHAPTER *Eleven*

Jackson pulled the car into the parking lot of a warehouse that appeared to have seen better days. When Jackson appointed Destiny his right hand on the team, Destiny visited all the places there were to visit. He showed her around and the ropes to the game. It was her first time being at the warehouse because nobody was allowed there besides him along with one other.

"What business is this?" Destiny side-eyed the establishment.

"It's my office. Come on. And please, enough questions." Jackson let Destiny out of the car. He closed the door behind her and started up the path to the back entrance with Destiny in tow.

"State your business here," a man wearing dark shades said. He appeared fresh out of a bodybuilding competition.

"State my business? Dude, this is my damn office, move

your big ass out of my way before I place some lead in you," Jackson complained.

"Nah, I can't do that." the man placed his hands in front of him as he looked down on Jackson like he was some average man that tried to be granted access.

Jackson pulled out his Glock and placed it to the man's forehead. "Don't make me put these bullets in your ass. You on my property. Move before I move you," Jackson threatened.

"Put the gun down, Jackson. You don't own anything, it's my property. But come in," a voice said over the intercom.

The bodyguard stepped aside and let Jackson and Destiny inside. As Jackson entered the building, he shoved the man into the steel door and mugged him.

"Better not happen again." Jackson fixed the collar of his suit and strolled into the building like the most important man on earth.

Destiny followed Jackson into the office without any questions, he made it clear back in the car that the questions had to stop until they were someplace else. The warehouse was all about business nothing less.

An older white man in a white suit stood up from behind the desk when the door opened. He fired up a cigar as he watched Jackson become undone.

"Sonny, what are you doing here?" Jackson fixed his tie as he approached Sonny.

"What am I doing here? I need a reason to come to

one of my properties." Sonny blew the smoke in Jackson's face.

"No, you don't. I was sayi—" Jackson cut off when he realized that Destiny had come with him. When he told her to tag along with him, he planned to hit up the warehouse to show her the ropes and how his crew handled shipments for out-of-state customers.

"Who the hell is this? And why the hell is she here while I'm here?" Sonny stared at Destiny for a moment, he took a drag of the cigar once more then blew the smoke at her.

"She's my girl. She helps me with the business. Have a nice head on her shoulders too." Jackson pulled Destiny to him.

"I don't give a fuck who she is. You know how I feel about new faces around me. I don't like new faces; new faces don't suppose to see me. Are you all sudden fucking dumb, Jackson?" Sonny slammed his hand against the desk.

"Sonny, I had no idea you would be here," Jackson said.

"Tell your little right-now chick or whatever the today's hoes are called to get out of here while we talk," Sonny demanded.

Destiny snapped her neck to the side and shot Sonny a deadly glare. "Oh, hell, nah. Who does this poppa smurf white mothfucka think he's talking to?"

Jackson grabbed Destiny by the arm. "Shut up! Don't ever disrespect him. Go outside and wait for me."

"Are you serious, Jackson?" Destiny couldn't believe how Jackson tucked his tail in the presence of Sonny. She wanted to see her man amped up and act a fool on Sonny for the disrespect.

"Very! Go wait in the car, baby girl. Please." Jackson shooed Destiny away.

"Fine!" Destiny turned on her heels and headed out of the office. But instead of going out to the car, she waited next to the door to see what was so important that she had to get out. Jackson never made her get out during business.

"Please don't bring hood rats around my business. She has no manners. We don't have time for extra drama. Too much is on our plates," Sonny fussed.

"She is not a hood rat. She is a dope woman. She is smart and a good businesswoman. Plus, did you see her?" Jackson defended Destiny's case to Sonny.

"I don't care how fine she is. She better not fuck up my money. You are so soft but then again that's your mom's fault. All I need you to do is run my business, not act like you are a rapper. You are still a white boy from the Valley." Sonny shot Jackson's confidence down like he'd always done when Jackson was a child. Sonny was the only father figure Jackson knew, so Jackson tried his best to live up to Sonny's expectations and not let him down because it would've been impossible to live with the guilt of not being enough.

"She won't. I got this. That's why you put me in charge. I know what I'm doing dad," Jackson said.

"You can be easily replaced." Sonny made it clear that

Jackson had no easy way in. It was strictly about business, and if that meant placing someone in Jackson's place, he was going to do exactly that.

"Replace me?" Jackson couldn't count on two hands how many times Sonny threatened to replace him.

"I will if my money keeps coming in slow. For you to have my drugs in the clubs, money isn't coming in quick and clean enough." Sonny took a seat behind the desk.

"Your priority is selling my product and cleaning my money." Sonny took a deep breath as disappointment overtook him while Jackson stood before him like a lost child.

"No one is stopping me from winning this election."

"I got it, Sonny. Look I got some money out in the car for you, a suitcase full." Jackson heard his heart in his ears.

"Only one briefcase? Yeah, you're losing your touch boy. I'm not who I am in this community from making small business moves. I'm the big fucking fish around here." Sonny massaged his temples and drew in a long inhale.

Sonny pressed a button on the desk. "Tony, bring in the work."

Destiny's heart sunk when Sonny's voice blared over the speaker. She darted out of the door, almost knocking the bodyguard on the ground. Once she was to the car she paced around as she thought about all the shit Jackson had been selling her about what he did and how he called the shots. It all made sense as she put it together.

"What in the fuck?" Destiny murmured.

From what she overheard, Sonny called the shots, he

was the man behind the operation, Jackson stood as a middleman, he had no real ties in the game. What he said didn't fly with anybody if it didn't go through Sonny.

Destiny leaned against the car as she saw Jackson walk towards her with two duffel bags that seemed to weigh a ton. She heard all she needed to know to realize what kind of man he was. Sonny walked all over him like he was nobody at all, and all he did was take it on the chin like some child who were incapable of defending himself.

"What the hell was that about?" Destiny snapped.

"He runs this shit all through the city. He is a multi-millionaire running for office." Jackson popped the trunk of the car, tossed the duffel bags in the trunk, and pulled out a briefcase.

"I thought you ran this. I thought I worked for you?" Destiny frowned.

"You are! But there is always a man above the man. I'm surprised you haven't seen him all over the TV." The way Jackson spoke after being in Sonny's presence made Destiny view him sideways.

"I don't watch TV." Destiny sighed.

"He does a lot for the city, especially the black community." Jackson tried his best to inform Destiny about Sonny's involvement with everything and how he pretty much ran the city.

Destiny frowned. "What the hell does that all mean?"

"It means he is the head white man in charge. You need to know that, so learn to keep your mouth shut."

Jackson leaned over and put his pointer finger in Destiny's face.

"I thought you were the white man in charge. Maybe I'm with the wrong white man," Destiny snapped.

Jackson grabbed Destiny by the throat and glared at her. "I have enough shit I'm dealing with than to stand here and deal with a disrespectful bitch like you. If you have a problem with the way things are being ran, then maybe you should take your ass back to the club."

Destiny pushed Jackson and broke away from the grip he had on her. "Don't you ever put your fucking hands back on me. While you were too busy doing heavens knows what, I was out there gettin' your money back from Manuel, something your scary white ass could never do. So, nigga don't think you can toss me around like that when I do shit out here in these streets that you can't."

"Just get in the car," Jackson demanded.

Destiny backed down from challenging Jackson and hopped in the car with a bitter taste in her mouth, with the information she picked up from eavesdropping on the conversation Sonny had with Jackson, she knew they were basically family. Jackson was Sonny's stepson, but she failed to wrap her mind around why Jackson seemed afraid of him.

Instead of going home to relieve the sitter of her duties with Dj, Destiny decided to head over to Teddy's club to pay Skye a visit since they hadn't chilled in a while. With all the new information she found out about Jackson and Sonny being in charge, she needed a sample of what her old life tasted like.

Since she been all in with Jackson, she'd been extending herself and making sure nobody tried to get over him the way they used to. She put herself in a situation that risked her safety for him and the money she knew he needed back in his possession.

"There she goes." Skye hopped up from the chair and hugged Destiny. For the last month, Destiny promised Skye bigger gigs and possible video shoots. One thing after the next presented itself and made it impossible for her to stay true to her word. Jackson placed a lot of responsibility on her plate.

"You know I had to come to see you. I've been trying to get out this way for a few weeks now. Atlanta to LA is killing me. Things are slowing up now though, I should be back caught up soon." Destiny took a seat in the old chair that used to be her spot in the dressing room, it had been months since she left, and nobody had shown up to take her spot.

"But I see that hoe couldn't find my replacement." Destiny laughed as she viewed her old makeup spot.

"Girl, word in the club is that Teddy is gettin' out in a few weeks. Joseline hasn't been keeping the club up how she was supposed to. I even heard she been stealing from Teddy; I doubt she even tried to find a replacement with all the sneaky shit she has going on." Skye secured her pink wig tightly on her head. She'd been experimenting with different looks for the crowd to get more money thrown at her on stage or make the men want her so bad they pay for a private section and hopefully a little more after that.

"Damn. I mean, it's not surprising. Joseline always seemed sneaky to me." Destiny viewed herself in the mirror, she looked different than she had months ago, she was all tired-looking and stressed. The life Jackson promised her, in the beginning, was nothing like she lived now. She had to get her hands dirty damn there every day, the money she had was due to her pulling her load not because of him breaking her off any bread.

"You on next. Get your ass out there and shake some ass and titties." Joseline peeped her head in the door without paying Destiny any attention, since she rolled with Jackson, Joseline made sure to steer clear of making beef between the two of them. She valued her life far too much than to get caught up with a dope pusher and his girl.

"I'm on my way." Skye threw her hands in the air to shoo Joseline away.

"I can't wait until you hook me the fuck up. I'm ready to be done with this shit here."

"I got you. I have a few other deals I need to line up. You're in there like gravy on rice," Destiny assured.

"I'm holding you to that shit," Skye removed herself from the seat and structed out the dressing room wearing an all-pink skimpy outfit that showcased her entire body like fine art. The gemstones sparkled in the light.

Destiny looked around to see if the dressing room was clear. She removed a small pack of cocaine from her bra and poured some on her fingertip. She brushed her finger across her gums and within minutes she saw doubles.

She used to be angry at Tammy for doing drugs, the shoes were on her feet now. She had become the person she hated most. Her life somehow shaped out like Tammy's, the only difference was that she had money to show, and she wasn't hooked to a crack pipe.

As the drug hit her system, Tammy briefly occupied Destiny's mind. She hadn't spoken to her mother since she moved out to Atlanta. Before Destiny left, they had a pretty good relationship, although Tammy did talk to her recklessly from time to time.

"I can't believe this." Destiny struggled out of the dressing room.

Whenever Jackson had her doing a drop, her hands somehow ended up in the product. She started off small, only doing a line every other week, then it turned into a daily thing, she couldn't get through life the way she used to without being high on some sort of substance.

"Umm, look who decided to show her face after being gone forever. Don't think you coming back here to get a job." Joseline bumped into Destiny in the main lobby. The cocaine had Destiny too gone to even think about going at Joseline for disrespect.

"What you too good to say something back?" Joseline

stopped in her tracks, usually she got a reaction out of Destiny, that night Destiny hadn't even summoned a word.

"Did you hear me?" Joseline's hands flew to her mouth when she viewed Destiny's eyes, they were unfocused and red. She'd been in the game long enough to know when someone was under drugs.

"You get with Jackson, he turns you out on that shit? Do you know what happens to people who get hooked? They end up on the streets with nothing to their name except an addiction." Joseline knew it wasn't her place to be in Destiny's business, she couldn't go to Jackson and read him his rights for pulling Destiny away from the club and getting her hooked on cocaine.

She was aware that he pushed drugs throughout the club, the dancers weren't allowed to touch it in her presence. What they did away from club was on them, long as they never stepped foot inside of the dressing room or on the stage high. She liked her dancers sober and aware of their surroundings, that had been Teddy's rule and a rule she decided to stick with.

"Mind your fucking business," Destiny slurred. She maneuvered through the club as she saw double, the view ahead was mingled with light and smoke, she peeped a glimpse of Skye on stage then everything went black.

The sun shined through the window as Destiny laid on Jackson's chest. One of Jackson's boys spotted Destiny in the club passed out, they immediately hit him up. He showed up within an hour to scoop her up. He had to put his business meeting on hold, to make sure she didn't end up abducted or laid up with a man who took advantage of her.

Skye waited with Destiny until Jackson showed. Joseline complained that Destiny made her club look bad, it wasn't anything new that people came into the club and got high, but the policy was for everyone to know their limits or never step back in the club.

But all Skye could worry about was if Destiny was good and how much substance took. The longest she'd been around Destiny in the club and outside of the club, Destiny never showed interest in any kind of strong substance expect plain Mary Jane.

Destiny removed herself from Jackson and sat on edge of the bed when her cell phone rung. She searched around the room making a mess of everything in her sight.

"Where did you put my phone, Jackson?" Destiny complained.

"I don't have your fucking phone, Destiny." Jackson pulled the covers over his head.

"I can't believe you got that fucked up last night and passed out. You messed up my plans."

"I told you earlier. I had too much to drink, that's it."

Destiny searched the room high and low until she laid eyes on her phone.

"If I find out you are dipping your hand in the product, I swear that's your ass," Jackson said.

"You really going to keep accusing me of that bullshit. Look, believe what you want to believe, Jackson." Destiny picked up her phone and fell to the floor, she had sixteen messages and two missed phone calls, the messages were all informing her that Tammy was found dead inside of her house the morning before, and the morgue needed to get in touch with her next to kin.

"Oh, God! This can't be true," Destiny pressed the phone against her chest as her soul seemed to peak out of her body.

"Fuck! I can't do this."

Jackson tossed the covers and charged over to Destiny. "What's wrong? What happened, Destiny?"

"It's my momma…she's dead." Destiny sobbed.

Jackson grabbed Destiny into his arms and allowed her to cry it out, for the period they'd been together, he never really heard her speak on Tammy or what it was like back home. Destiny kept that part of life in the dark, and since she never talked about it, he figured, it wasn't important.

"I should've been there. I didn't do enough for her."

All the pain Destiny endured back home suddenly had become nonexistent, all she saw Tammy as was her mother, her mother who'd left her in the cold world. And Destiny thought, maybe that was the first step of grief, the part of being in denial and suddenly forgetting all the pain the person caused while they were on earth. Then she figured maybe none of that even mattered, Tammy was gone now, she couldn't fuss with her anymore or be angry about what had transpired over the years.

"Don't do that. Don't blame yourself for anything," Jackson said.

"But I should've been there." Destiny removed herself from the floor and staggered to the bathroom, the high from the night before nagged at her at the base of her forehead and temples.

"Let me know if you need anything for the arrangements," Jackson said.

"Okay," Destiny leaned over the bathroom sink and sobbed a bit more.

She hadn't any real close friends back home that could comfort her when she made it back. Shirell and her wasn't speaking, nobody outside of the people who witnessed her deal with Tammy over the years was going to feel her pain or understand it.

"You got this, Destiny." Destiny slid to the floor.

Her entire life fell from underneath, then it hit her, Dj had received the same mother as her. She wasn't ever home like Tammy, and then she had gotten hooked on drugs in the process. Reality kicked in and made her see that she was heading down a path far worse than Tammy.

Destiny picked up the phone and called Shirell, she was the only person who knew the trauma she had experienced. Her one best friend, Dominique, folded and went after D. Wallace and hooked him with children and marriage.

"You okay?" Shirell heart skipped as she answered the phone.

Destiny hadn't spoken to her in months, and the only way she was able to see Dj was if she popped up at his school, and he'd told Shirell that he didn't see Destiny for days at a time and some woman kept him while she was away.

"Is everything okay with Dj, he's not sick, is he?"

"No, it's not Dj. He's fine." Destiny held the phone a moment to gather her thoughts. "It's…my momma is dead. They found her dead inside of the house yesterday, and I have to go out there to make funeral arrangements." Destiny knew Tammy would end up dead someday, she lived a hard life, and refused to go to rehab. She hadn't prepared herself for when it happened or would've thought that when she died, she would be battling her addiction to drugs and money.

"Ohh, Destiny. I'm sorry to hear that. I know it's hard on you right now and can't anyone understand your pain the way you do, but it's going to be okay. It will be hard, but you will find a way to get through it." Shirell knew what it felt like to lose a parent.

"I want to apologize for being a suck ass friend. I really thought I was doing my best with Dj." Destiny broke down harder on the phone, Tammy's passing hit her in places she never knew death could hit a person.

"Shirell I really fucked up. I'm in a fucked up place in

my life right now. I'm no better than Tammy, I don't spend time with my child. Sometimes I look at him and wonder why I kept him if I can't be the mother he needs?"

"Destiny, process one thing at a time. Right now, focus on getting through having to go back to Memphis for the arrangements, then when you get back here, you can start to pick your life back up and head in the right direction." Shirell took a long exhale.

She figured she and Destiny wouldn't ever speak again, that she would have to forever sneak around the city to check up on Dj to ensure he was being somewhat taken care of. Destiny hit her up and broke down, she didn't have anybody else that cared like Shirell cared, not Skye, Ashley or even Jackson; Nobody in Atlanta knew her entire story except Shirell. Everybody else only knew pieces of the story, the pieces she was willing to share without feeling judged.

"Yeah, you're right." Destiny wiped her tears away.

"I know this is a pretty fucked up time to ask you to do anything for me. But please, watch Dj for me while I head out to Memphis. I have a sitter that you can use if you have any plans. I really need you to watch him for me, okay?" Destiny pulled the pack of coke from her bra, she closed the bathroom door and locked it to keep Jackson away from the view of her getting high.

"Take care of him, okay?"

"Destiny, I would love to watch him. Just be careful, okay? And don't get into any trouble."

Shirell was aware that Dominique and D. Wallace lived

in Memphis together and was married with children, she found it out over a year ago, she never mentioned it to Destiny though, because she knew that kind of information wasn't something she should relay. She figured it was best if Destiny somehow found it out on her own.

"Thank you, Shirell. I really owe you for putting up with me this long. You're really the only true friend I've ever had," Destiny confessed.

"You're welcome, D..." Shirell held the phone. "...Send me where to pick him up from and I'll be on my way."

"Alright." Destiny ended the call and stared at the coke in her hand.

Tammy's death gave her every reason to flush it down the toilet, yet every reason not to. She had emotions built inside that she refused to deal with right away. She had to take a flight back home to bury her mother with the anxiety of possibly bumping into Dominique and D. Wallace.

Destiny poked her finger in the bag and rubbed the cocaine on her top gums then she broke down in sobs again. She leaned against the wall, everything seemed to go black except the pain. The pain still nudged at her and tugged at her heart. If she wanted the pain to subside completely, she had to do a bit more than what she originally took. However, taking more meant she would be unconscious and unable to go meet up with Shirell or catch a plane later.

"Yo, Destiny. I'm sorry about your mom," Jackson said

from the other side of the door.

"I still need your head in the game though. You have to run two loads today."

"Find someone else to fucking do it. I have to find a flight back home," Destiny yelled as she hit her fist against the door. Even the number of drugs she consumed couldn't suppress the rage she felt.

Jackson was selfish like all the other men she had in her life, they all cared about themselves and what they could gain. Nobody ever seemed to see her, to see her pain and hold space in their heart for her.

"Look, you knew what you signed up for. It's sad, she died or whatever, I still have business to run, and you still have responsibility," Jackson said firmly.

"Fuck you, you stupid heartless mothafucka. I said, find someone else to do it." Destiny tucked the pack of coke away and opened the door.

"Are you out of your mind? You don't dare open your mouth to talk to me like that again. I gave you this life and I can take it all away with the snap of my finger. Don't forget about the hand that help feed you. Now, like I said, you have work to do." Jackson ended the conversation there and headed out to get his day started.

Destiny thought about doing the whole pack of coke and forgetting about everything that needed her present. She still had arrangements to make, to get Dj over to Shirell, do drops for Jackson, all of it seemed next to impossible to complete while grief lied dormant in her heart.

CHAPTER Twelve

The news of Tammy being dead was three days in the past for Destiny, she managed to get through the bit of work Jackson had lined up and Dj was with Shirell until she arrived back to Atlanta to Memphis. Days ago, it seemed like she couldn't even think straight now all she was doing was thinking and hadn't had any type of substances to keep her leveled.

"I guess you can pretty much throw all this shit in the garbage," Destiny's aunt Wanda said.

Wanda didn't live in Memphis she moved to Kansas before Destiny was old enough to walk. Destiny had only saw her once as a child. Wanda didn't lead a easy life either but she hadn't chosen the same destructive path as Tammy.

When things were bad at home, Destiny tried to get in touch with Wanda, left her countless voice messages, all the calls were unreturned. Destiny figured she was a lost cause and not even Wanda wanted to deal with the daughter of some addict. Nobody in the family wanted to take her in or force Tammy to get any help. Now that Tammy was dead, there stood Wanda, telling Destiny what to do with the few items that belonged to Tammy.

"It meant something to her. I should probably place it in storage." Destiny viewed the home she grew up in. It wasn't anything close to top tier when she lived there, it wasn't anything close to a living environment by then either.

"Place in storage for what? This shit smells like someone sat their open ass on it for weeks at a time. All that dusty ass shit she has in her room needs to be burned. I'm not going through anything in here, it's like if you touch anything you prone to catch a disease," Wanda spoke with her hand over her nose.

"If you want to dig through this shit then have at it, I won't be of service."

"Bitch I never asked you to be of any service to me. I did this shit alone while you were somewhere busy with your life. The addiction Tammy had, I dealt with it and saw it through. The emotional abuse, I had to endure it. When the lights got cut off because she chose to feed her addiction rather than pay the light bills, I was the one who had to sleep in the cold." Destiny pointed her finger in Wanda's face.

"You didn't give a fuck then what make you think I want you to now? You don't even have to show your face at her funeral. Get back on a plane and take your selfish ass back where you came from. Because I sure as hell don't need you."

"I will be at the hotel." Wanda turned on her heels and left out the house.

Destiny walked down the hallway and instantly fell sick, the task itself seemed like it would be impossible. Going through Tammy's things to see what was salvageable was a task that wasn't for the weak. The thought did cross her mind that Wanda had been right, she didn't want to give the satisfaction though. Wanda couldn't have known what was best. Tammy lacked all kinds of things, Destiny, however, knew that Tammy wouldn't want all her items tossed out on the curved or burned to ashes.

Destiny searched the house high and low to see what she could save in remembrance of Tammy, the more she searched, the more she saw that Tammy really had been poor and had sold everything of importance to afford her addiction.

Destiny headed into the room she used to occupy and took a seat on the bed, she looked around the room and pondered on all the times she cried herself to sleep due to Tammy's negligence as a parent. Her thoughts of Tammy's shortcomings hit her soul; she wondered how many nights he cried for her to be there for him. How much he must've missed her while she was busy trying to make a living selfishly.

The more money she touched, the more it wasn't enough. Her values in life went up, she wanted finer things out of life and for Dj to have all the things she never had. But she wasn't giving him the mother she never experienced, she in return gave him the same mother she had in a better living environment.

After Destiny couldn't find anything worth holding onto with Tammy, she headed out and took a stroll around the neighborhood in nostalgia. Once the whole nostalgic made her sick, she headed downtown to her hotel at the Four Seasons. Last time she was there, it was all thanks to D. Wallace, and he had her mind blown that night. She'd never stepped foot inside of something that looked so fancy, now she was used to the fancy living and could afford anything she wanted, and wasn't due to her being some WNBA player or the first lady of a baller. She got her money out of the mud.

Destiny dialed up Shirell to check on Dj and see how things were going since she was miles away from home. Plus, she had a few hours before she had to be at the funeral home to finalize the arrangements, so she had a few hours to waste.

"I was calling to check on you two?" Destiny started. She thought about telling Shirell about the encounter with Wanda and her plans to toss all Tammy's items to the curve.

"Girl we're fine, Dj just finished up with his homework now he's in the living room having a snack and watching some crazy cartoon that he insists on me watching with him," Shirell said.

"Oh, that's cute. I really do thank you for loving him

the way you do," Destiny sighed.

She and Shirell weren't in the best place in their friendship. Shirell made it seem like they hadn't missed a beat. She was somehow back in the swing of looking after Dj and carrying some of Destiny's burdens on her back.

"So, how's things going out that way?" Shirell asked.

"It's going," Destiny replied as she viewed the city from the window. As she stood there, she felt eighteen again, young and dumb and thinking life was going to start with being D. Wallace's woman.

"Why do I have this feeling that you're not telling me what's going on?" Shirell said.

Destiny leaned against the window as her life flashed before her, it was her having to deal with Wanda alone, being back in Memphis where her life went to shit, then the whole Domonique and D. Wallace situation. She kept going over in her mind what she would do if she ran into them, she assumed she would see them and hide until the coast was clear or see them and speak and pretend to not care. There were many ways the situation could've played out and Destiny made sure she visited each scenario properly.

"I don't want to bother you with all the petty drama, you already have your hands full enough with Dj." Destiny fell back from laying any more burden on Shirell. As she done so, she thought about why Shirell never lived her life fully, what was Shirell holding back from her.

"Girl, stop. You know I don't mind," Shirell said.

"Oh, shit. My food has arrived, I'll call you back later

to check in after I stop by the funeral home." Destiny ended the call without any interruptions from the door. She hadn't ordered any room service, she only made up an excuse to get off the phone with Shirell, so she wouldn't have to go into details about the trip.

Destiny laid around in the room until the evening, then she found the strength to drive back down to the other side of the city to the funeral home. She knew Tammy wasn't in any kind of life insurance and that the cost of the funeral would be on her. When she was on the phone the funeral director told her that it would be cheaper not to have a funeral and to get Tammy cremated. Something about Tammy's body being burned to ash didn't sit right with Destiny. However, it did make sense since nobody in the city cared for Tammy; wasn't anybody going to be up in the church saying she was a good woman who loved and cared for people.

The only thing people remembered about Tammy by then was being on the street corner begging for money to buy drugs. She was nobody special not even to Destiny, if she decided to speak at the funeral, she wasn't even sure what she would choose to say about Tammy. She did remember some good years, but the bad years outweighed the good, so they didn't truly matter anymore.

"Glad you could make it out here," Yolanda greeted Destiny.

Destiny chose the closest funeral home to where tammy lived, since it was close by, maybe people would come show respect because they saw a funeral in session.

Yolanda was a heavy-set woman with a face that even a grandmother wouldn't be proud of. Her hair was tied up in a tight bond with her edges receding. "You really didn't have to come out this way. You could've chosen the cremation route and I would've shipped her remains out there to you."

"Yeah, I thought about going that route. The whole fire, her body burning to only ash, spooked me a bit. I wouldn't want my son to do that to me, and I wouldn't want to do that to Tammy." Destiny followed Yolanda up to the front of the church.

"The way Tammy lived, I thought it best to cremate her. Lord direct my steps, but a funeral for a junkie is a waste of money. I knew Tammy, well, she didn't have many friends and her family scattered all over the place. You could've saved that money." Yolanda tried her best to keep it professional like a church going saint. She married a preacher a few years back and changed her entire life around. Back in the day, she used to be on drugs with Tammy, Destiny saw her around the block a few times begging for change.

"So, does that mean you should be cremated when you die too? I remember you, Yolanda. You used to be on my momma's stoop smoking that shit and, on the corners, begging for money to get high." Destiny looked sideways at Yolanda.

"Watch your mouth in the Lord's house. I repented for my sins. Jesus forgave me and said, 'this is your clean slate', and I didn't sin no more. I begged God to redirect my steps and he did that." Yolanda poked her chest out as the words moved her soul.

"I'm saying, it's not your place to judge anybody. Don't forget where you come from before you try to throw somebody out to the wolves. Tammy may not have been a friend to anybody, she was still a person." Destiny thought she would never see the day of her defending Tammy.

Tammy threw her out to drown as a child. Destiny went from house to house to get a meal throughout the week after school. Then when Dominique started inviting her over for dinner, life suddenly became easier on her end. She didn't have to beg anybody for food, that's how she really started to trust Domonique. Then Dominique wanted to control her life. She told whom she could hang out with, but she never directly told her. She had a problem with any new person that walked into Destiny's life. She couldn't get Destiny away from Shirell though. Destiny found another friend when she landed on Shirell's path, they had aspirations that were close in life, and if Destiny could rewind time, she would've been closer to Shirell and allowed her to influence her more rather being out with Dominique trying to bag a baller.

"No, you're right. And it wasn't right for me to throw her under the bus like that. But some heartaches are meant to be mended in different ways. Tammy wasn't very good to you, and I tried to save you the trouble of having to see her this way," empathy suddenly filled Yolanda's tone.

"You shouldn't have had to come all this way to lay her to rest. I know the Lord says to forgive but Tammy put you through some really bad things that you still probably need to heal from, and it was out of my good heart that I tried to save you the pain of laying her to rest. Not everybody needs a funeral, you know."

"What kind of sideways apology was that?" Destiny shook her head in disbelief of the way Yolanda acted.

It was always the people who claimed they were saved who forgot where they had come from. They were worse than the people who were on the street and beating the streets every day. The way Destiny saw, wasn't any sin bigger than the next. Yolanda could've busted hell wide open by judging another since God looked high and saw in the lowest slums.

"Can you take me to her body and leave me for a while?" Destiny asked.

"Okay, that's fine." Destiny thought the planning of a funeral was all love and support and that the people who directed the funeral was supposed to make the load a bit easier by granting certain request of the grieving, she had been wrong.

"Follow me." Yolanda structed down the hallway, then took a left and they went down another hallway, until they reached a blue door at the end of the second hallway.

"I got her all cleaned up, since I knew you would be out here. I still need to do her hair and makeup. Right now, she look like… I don't even know." Yolanda walked over to a freezer and pulled Tammy's body out. "She can't stay out too long, make sure it's a quick visit."

"Thank you." Destiny summoned.

Destiny hadn't laid eyes on Tammy in years, hadn't even saw a picture of her. She did speak to her briefly a few times over the years. During most of the calls Tammy asked for money and Destiny told her there was nothing she could do except pay a bill or two. There was no way she would put money in Tammy's hand knowing that it was only going to be used towards drugs. She saw what Tammy did with money and how she blew it on the stupidest shit.

"Why couldn't you choose me? Why wasn't I enough for you to get clean and live your life right, Momma?" Destiny grabbed hold of Tammy's cold hand and sobbed. "All I wanted was for you to be there, to be proud of me. I only wanted a momma." Seeing the way Tammy parented, impacted Destiny more than she claimed. She didn't want to be like Tammy, yet she had deep scars that made her worse in some ways. Dj suffered from her negligence, but he at least had somebody like Shirell there to pick him up when he felt alone.

"I love you, Momma. Even though I have every reason to hate you." Destiny wiped her eyes and turned away from Tammy.

She told Yolanda to put the body back up. They then discussed more arrangements which didn't involve a lot. Tammy was going to have a small funeral with a few family members and close friends from back in the day. Destiny made sure nobody let the junkies in the church, Tammy hung out with enough of them while she was alive, she saw no sense in them being around her dead body too.

Once they lowered Tammy into the ground, Destiny stayed at the gravesite for a while. It was hard to come to terms with that being the last time she would ever see her mother's body in the flesh. Then she knew now that the funeral was behind her, she had to be back on the plane to Atlanta where her real life was at. Please Jackson, take care of Dj better and be a better friend to Shirell. She wondered though, what would it cost her to get away from the life that Jackson swindled her into.

"I'm sorry about what happened to Tammy. I used to stop over there to give her some food occasionally." Destiny turned in the direction the familiar voice came from. Her veins went cold like she was in the dead of Winter.

Dominique looked older, not too older. She didn't resemble the hoodrat she'd been when she and Destiny were friends. She was dressed in a designer suit with some high heels. Her hair was cut shorter than the way she used to wear it.

"I know it's been forever, and we lost contact, but I still thought I should look out for your momma. Not that I was obligated. Tammy never liked me, I think I did earn her points after I showed my face and helped her over the years. She was really trying to get clean." Dominique looked down at the fresh dirt rather than up at Destiny. "She told me, you cut ties with her and never came to visit."

"Dominique why are you even talking to me right now? I have nothing to say to your trifling ass. While you were swinging your long pussy across the city to my momma, maybe you should've told your nigga to be active in his son's life. Y'all playing this perfect family bullshit, then step the fuck up and give my son what's owed to him." Destiny viewed Dominque in tears. She hadn't faced Dominque in years, never got the chance to beat the brakes off her for sleeping with D. Wallace right after she gave birth to Dj.

"Take care of a child that he didn't want to begin with? He told you what to do with the child, you were the one who threw your entire career away and had a baby. You thought that was going to keep him—it didn't and he fell right in my hands. I never pressured him. He became the man I needed him to be because he cared about me unlike he cared for you." Domonique folded her arms without backing down from Destiny. She never been the kind of person to tuck her tail and hide from another. She always shot it to Destiny straight and wasn't going to stop now that she was married to D. Wallace. She lived on the other side of the city with the housewives, yet she still rolled in the mud whenever she had to.

"You know what, I don't know why I'm even wasting my breath on a stupid bitch like you anyway. You only up because you with a nigga. I got mine out the mud and living my best fucking life in Atlanta. My son doesn't want for shit, hadn't even asked about his daddy since he been in the world. You aren't worth fifteen cents without D.

Wallace. Now bitch step before I break my legs off in your ass!" Destiny said.

"Whatever, I wanted to let you know that Tammy needed you and you wasn't there. The way D. Wallace wanted you, but you did some stupid shit. They both ended up in good care and you can thank me for that." Dominique strutted off.

Destiny took a steady inhale as she watched Dominque walk away like she'd won a war. Destiny ran after Dominique and jumped on her back. They stumbled to the ground and rolled down the steep hills until a tombstone stopped them. Destiny got on top of Dominique, she punched her in the face and slammed her head into a tombstone. Dominique tried to grabbed Destiny's hair but failed. Destiny wrapped her hands around Dominique's throat! The death that crept into Dominique's eyes made adrenaline flood Destiny's veins.

"You see, I've always been that bitch. And will forever be. I can take your life right now and you can join Tammy since you two were close." Destiny refused to loosen the grip she held around Dominique's throat, not until she heard her phone going off with text alerts. Destiny rolled off Dominique and viewed the sky; the clouds were grey and rolling quickly. Droplets of rain poured down as lightning overtook the sky.

"Live to fight another day, bitch." Destiny removed herself from the ground. She grabbed her phone out of her purse. Her heart sunk with the ton of unread text messages. They were all from Jackson.

Destiny quickly dialed Jackson with a lump of vomit in her throat. "What do you mean they're gone?"

Jackson paced around the warehouse. "He hit me up and told me that you're going to pay for crossing him the way you did."

"Manuel?" Destiny questioned.

When she showed up at Manuel's club, she was supposed to have a meeting with him about the payment, not force him to up the money. Jackson told her to pick up what he had to offer, he wasn't worried about the whole tab being paid in full, because the clubs being in debt meant he could do whatever whenever, he always used it as collateral.

"Yeah, Manuel! I told you to pick up what he had and bounce. You pulled a gun on him, you threatened him. You made trouble for you and my team," Jackson fussed.

"What the fuck you mean, I made trouble? I was trying to help you. You were the one too pussy to get involved. You allow these niggas to walk all over you." Destiny couldn't even think straight.

"Well, he's about to walk all over you. He has your friend and your son. You better hope she's good enough to fuck then maybe he won't slice her throat. As for your son, you better have enough money to buy him back." Jackson ended the call.

Destiny looked around at Dominique as her heart shrunk the size of a pea. She had to get her son back one way or another, and if she wanted to make sure Shirell got back home to safety too, then she had to take matters into her own hand and think the plan out thoroughly. D. Wallace was an NBA player who lived on the rich side of Memphis, he owed her for Dj and even if he did give her the money he owed her, it wasn't going to be enough to buy Dj out of trouble.

"You owe me." Destiny wiped her tears as she aimed her pistol at Dominique.

"Oh, shit." Dominique covered her face. "Destiny put that gun away we can talk about this. We can talk all this shit through. I'm sorry, okay. I'm sorry that I did you dirty. If it makes you feel any better, D isn't ever home, he has other children across the country and he has another child on the way with a woman he cheated on me with several more times after I found out about it." Dominique spilled her entire heart to Destiny.

"I don't give a fuck about all of that. You owe me and D. Wallace owe me. I want you to wire one million dollars to my account right now," Destiny demanded.

Destiny figured she was overstepping herself demanding that amount of money, he probably didn't even owe that much if she would've stuck him for child support. It was either go big or fly back to Atlanta and pray she was able to make a deal with Manuel without money being involved.

"One million dollars? Are you insane?" Dominique couldn't see Destiny clearly due to the tears that clouded her vision.

"He will kill me."

"I mean, it's going to be, I kill you right here, so choose

wisely." Destiny held the pistol tighter as her finger got happy around the trigger. She'd gotten herself deep in the drug game with Jackson, she made one wrong step and Manuel ended her life, Shirell's life and possible Dj's.

"What happened to you?" Dominique held her head as she tried to stop the blood from oozing.

"This isn't you. It's not like you. Destiny, what happened? I don't understand."

"Enough with the questions, log into your bank and wire the money," Destiny demanded.

"I don't even think I have my account set up that way. I never had to wire anybody money before."

Dominique tried to think of a million ways on how to get herself out of the situation with Destiny. D. Wallace was nowhere in sight, there weren't anybody out in the graveyard anymore, the people who were at the funeral was all long gone. She got herself into a situation that only money was able to buy her out of.

"I don't even think they allow that amount of money to be wired from a mobile app. We'll have to go to the bank." Dominique hoped that the idea of going to that bank would scare Destiny.

"Then I guess we're going to the bank." Destiny snatched Dominique up by the arm.

"Destiny, I have children that need me. I can't die like this." Dominique sobbed.

"Then I guess you better cooperate. You give me the money, I will be out of your way and back across the country," Destiny said.

"Okay, listen to me. I see D. Wallace make withdrawals all the time, when you go to the bank and request that much, they have to report it, and people in high places come and ask a lot of questions. Back at home, D. Wallace has one hundred thousand in cash, there are diamonds too I'm sure that's worth at least half a million dollars. I know it's not the million you wanted, it's at least something without people having to be involved," Dominique said.

"How do I know I can trust you?" Destiny asked.

"You don't know. But it sounds like you're in some deep shit, so you have no other option. Like you said, I owe you for being a shitty friend. And since D isn't acting right, I don't care who get hands on his money, long as it's not taking anything out of my pocket. The house, the cars, the restaurant and franchises are what I'm after when I file for divorce." Dominique spoke on the divorce like she'd thought about since the first day they exchanged vows.

Before they even got married, D. Wallace wanted Dominique to sign a prenup, and Dominique agreed without hesitation because she knew that if she didn't act like she wanted his money, then he wouldn't make her sign anything and the whole prenup idea would be tossed out the window. That's exactly what happened. She earned D. Wallace's trust, he married her without making her sign any prenup, so now she could take him for half of everything or possibly more.

"You've always been a dirty bitch." Destiny smirked.

"And that's why we were friends because somebody has

to be shiesty to get ahead in the world. We can't all play fair," Dominique replied.

"Alright, let's go." Destiny waved the gun and Dominique walked ahead.

Destiny had a renal, she wasn't worried about leaving the car at the graveyard. The dealer was eventually going to find it. She grabbed her luggage out of the trunk and transferred it into Dominique's backseat.

Dominique upgraded over the years, she had a Land Rover the last time Destiny saw her, now she had an all-black G Wagon with peanut butter interior. Destiny couldn't help but to take the luxury of the G Wagon in. She, too had upgraded her ride, it wasn't as expensive as Dominique's whip, but it wasn't cheap either. She had a burgundy Jaguar that she paid cash for after being in good with Jackson, plus the money she had saved up from the club as a dancer.

"I see another nigga upgraded your ride," Destiny said as she kept the pistol pointed to the back of Dominique's head.

"Actually, I bought this myself. I own two stores on the upper side of city. I know how to get my own now. I don't solely depend on D. Wallace anymore," Dominique said as she viewed Destiny in the rearview mirror.

"What have you gotten yourself in, Destiny? It sounded like it was serious."

"Don't pretend to care, now drive, bitch." Destiny demanded.

"Okay." Dominique started the engine and put the

gear in drive. She tried her best to drive without fearing Destiny blowing her brains out all over the interior.

"Oh, this is a nice home you have here," Destiny complimented. There was no doubt that Dominique picked it out and decorated herself, it looked like her style and taste in items.

"Thank you, I picked it out and did all the décor myself," Dominique said.

"Yeah, I figured you did," Destiny rolled her eyes.

"Can you hurry up? I need to be on the road." Destiny changed her flight times and booked a flight for later that night. With the way Manuel was moving, she couldn't put it past him that he had some of his crew waiting at the airport for her to arrive.

Dominique quickly put the money and diamonds in a suitcase and rolled it over to Destiny. "I really would like to catch up. I am sorry about Tammy. I pray everything works out for you, Destiny." Dominique gave a sympathetic expression.

Destiny gave a sly smile; she raised the pistol and shot Dominique in the left shoulder. "No, need to catch up. We're even now."

Dominique right hand instantly flew to her shoulder, and she fell to the floor in tears. A burning sensation overtook her shoulder and traveled to her chest. She thought cooperating with Destiny would somehow give her some points and remove her from the hot seat, but all it did was get her shot.

"Oh, fuck, you shot me. You shot me," Dominique welled.

"Suck it up. You'll live. Now you can brag on how D. Wallace baby momma ran up in your house and robbed you then shot you for no reason at all. Add it to your list of stories, don't leave out the part that I'll be back too. But if you give my name up to the cops, I'll be back to kill you and toss your children in the Mississippi River." Destiny tucked the gun away and walked out of the room. She grabbed the keys to Dominique's G Wagon and headed out the house.

Destiny tossed the suitcase on the passenger seat and circled around to the driver's side. She adjusted the rearview and viewed herself a moment. Then she called Jackson, he hadn't called her since she was at the graveyard trying to set things straight with Dominique.

"You better be calling to tell me that you back in the city?" Jackson said.

"No, but I'll be back soon." Destiny held the phone for a minute.

"I have money to pay Manuel off. I know it's money he wants. Why else would he take the two people that means the world to me?"

"You better hope it's money that he wants. Manuel sometimes wants blood for treason," Jackson said.

"Then I'll paint the city red behind mine. I be damn if

I let an old washed-up El Chapo want-to-be scare me. He has my son and my best friend." Destiny felt her heart turn cold, she had to make sure she took her feelings out of the situation.

"You talk big shit for somebody who should be afraid. You don't know how deep you dug yourself under, and you got me in a whole lot of shit too. My dad is trying to win an election, he doesn't need this kind of shit right now." Jackson took a drag of the blunt before he continued.

"After this is over, I'll have to drop you."

"Drop me? How the fuck you going to drop me?" Destiny leaned back in the seat.

"Aight, say less." Destiny ended the call.

She refused for another man to drop her when times got hard, she had to be in control of every situation if she wanted to survive and like Manuel was going to feel her, Jackson was going to feel her too. The entire city of Atlanta was going to feel whenever she came through and pained the sky red.

"You can't fuckin' drop me if I take over your entire team. You taught me all I needed to know bitch ass nigga. Now watch me overtake your empire." Destiny yelled as she backed out of the driveway. She did anything shiesty long as she been alive, but she remembered what Dominique said, *sometimes you have to be shiesty to get ahead.*

To be continued....

FROM THE WRITERS OF THE KILL G SECRET
BRITTANY LUCIO
BLUE KIMBLE
Finding
DESTINY
TAPOO PRODUCTIONS PRESENTS A FILM BY SHEENA HEROD " SHE SHE "
WRITTEN BY SHEENA HEROD STARRING BRITTANY LUCIO BLUE KIMBLE CURTIS WASHINGTON TOWANDA BRAXTON DON BRUMFIELD LYRIC BELLEZA
PRODUCED BY SHEENA HEROD AMANDA SHELBY & TONI BROOKS DIRECTED BY SHEENA HEROD

CPSIA information can be obtained
at www.ICGtesting.com
Printed in the USA
LVHW040721100723
751942LV00039B/331